Rise to Power 3

Lock Down Publications and Ca$h
Presents

Rise to Power 3

A Novel by *T.J. Edwards*

Lock Down Publications

P.O. Box 870494
Mesquite, Tx 75187

Lock Down Publications
Like our page on Facebook: Lock Down Publications @
www.facebook.com/lockdownpublications.ldp
Cover design and layout by: **Dynasty Cover Me**
Book interior design by: **Shawn Walker**
Edited by: **Kiera Northington**

Stay Connected with Us!

Text **LOCKDOWN** to 22828 to stay up-to-date with new releases, sneak peaks, contests and more…

Thank you!

Submission Guideline.

Submit the first three chapters of your completed manuscript to ldpsubmissions@gmail.com, subject line: Your book's title. The manuscript must be in a .doc file and sent as an attachment. Document should be in Times New Roman, double spaced and in size 12 font. Also, provide your synopsis and full contact information. If sending multiple submissions, they must each be in a separate email.

Have a story but no way to send it electronically? You can still submit to LDP/Ca$h Presents. Send in the first three chapters, written or typed, of your completed manuscript to:

LDP: Submissions Dept
Po Box 870494
Mesquite, Tx 75187

DO NOT send original manuscript. Must be a duplicate.

Provide your synopsis and a cover letter containing your full contact information.

Thanks for considering LDP and Ca$h Presents.

T.J. Edwards

Chapter 1

Ajani slid the brass knuckles onto his fingers and fixed them so they fit properly. He cocked back his arm, came forward with brute force and slammed his fist into the dread head's face, breaking his nose. I could even hear it snap. "One more time, nigga, who do you work for, and why the fuck are y'all airing at my cousin's funeral? Speak!"

I kept the flame of my blowtorch on the blade of the butter knife. It was already bright red. I couldn't wait to use it. The dread head tried to catch his breath. His nose was bent awkwardly, blood oozed out of both of his nostrils and down to his chin. He swallowed. "Mi work fah Damian, mon. He's yer wurst nightmare, and not somebody to play wiff. I follow orders or lose the life of mii family. What would you do?" he asked with his face all shiny with blood.

"What the nigga want wit me, Blood?" I asked and stepped in front of him with the red-hot butter knife. I wasn't expecting him to talk so easily. Now I was regretting lighting the knife up.

"You killed a bunch of the queens from Kingston, mon. You gotta pay for yer sins. It's the Jamaican way. No way around it. He'll get you sooner or later. Damian always does."

Ajani smacked the shit out of him for no reason. "Bitch nigga, where can we find this fool at? I need addresses, home, offices, his bitch cribs, everything. You already got that irritating ass accent. Choking on all that blood and shit is only making the communicating process worse." I mugged him, confused. Wondering, was my cousin out of his mind or what?

"Yo, where is this nigga's headquarters?" The dread head swallowed his blood and shrugged his shoulders. We had him tied to a chair in one of my trap's basements in Brooklyn.

"I tell you anything and they wipe out my entire family back in Jamaica. Mi can't risk it. Rather die as a mon than as a coward. I've said enuff already." He swallowed again and struggled to breathe through his broken nose. Now I was happy. I placed the flame of the torch back on to the butter knife until it turned red. Then sat the canister down, and slowly applied it to the side of his cheek. It sizzled and smelled like bacon. Smoke came from it. He screamed at the top of his lungs and Ajani burst out laughing as if he were at a comedy club.

"Where the fuck can I find him!" He hopped around in his chair, crying. When I pulled the butter knife back, it had his skin stuck to it. I could see the meat on his face. It was white, before the blood started to pour out of it.

"Fucking kill me now! Kahn't take dis pain. Kill me, ya bumbaclots ! Amerikins, mii don't fuck wit ya pussy—" I lit the knife again and placed the flaming blade right on his fore-head. Pressed it hard against him, and drug it downward. It sunk into his flesh like butter. I allowed for it to rest and burn him right under his right eye. His cheek had smoke drifting to the sky. Now he was really going hysterical. "Argh! Argh! Mii kahn't snitch! He'd kill mii whole family. Juss kill mii! Kill mii now!"

"Yo, burn his ass again. He think we playing wit him or somethin'," Ajani said, with his upper lip curled. He took a step back and kicked the dread head in the chest so hard that he flipped over in the chair and wound up on his side, bleeding.

When I went to reach for the canister, Ajani picked it up and started the flame. He knelt and grabbed a handful of the shooter's dreads, starting the flame. "Say, my nigga, if you don't tell us what we need to know, I'm about to burn yo ass like Lucifer. Start talking."

The Jamaican wheezed through his nose, struggling to breathe, blood puddling around him. "He got a spot a few blocks from the docks, right along the Delaware River. Most of his hoods operate out of the alley in Jersey. Now kill me. Kill me now, and make sure dat he knows I'm dead. Else he'll kill ma family fer mii snitching."

He turned onto his back. Ajani looked up at me. "You believe this nigga, Cuz?" I looked down on him for a long time, watching him squirm. Blood gushed out of every wound in his body. I felt no remorse for his bitch ass. Started to imagine one of those bullets he spit hitting my mother, daughter, or Bree and Rayven. That pissed me off worse than before.

"Yeah, Blood. Smoke this nigga, kid. And toss his ass in the harbor. Word up."

Ajani stood up. "You ain't said nothing but a word. But then, we about to go handle this Jamaican fuck nigga, right?" he asked, raising his Timb about knee high, then brought it down as hard as he could into the dread head's jaw, crushing it to the ground. The dread head seemed to bark like a dog as his face was crushed into the basement concrete. Ajani raised his Timb and stomped him over and over. Each time, he put a little more force into his stomps. By the time he finished, he'd completely smashed the dread's face inward. He lay on the floor dead-dead.

* * *

Rayven paced back and forth with a glass full of red wine. "We gotta get you some protection, Kaleb. Ain't no telling what them Jamaicans are on right now. And then, we gotta deal with Buddy. That nigga been missing in action for weeks now. I'm wondering when he's going to pop up and when he does, what he's going to be on? I think we need to get the fuck out of New York. Ain't no sense in us being here any longer. It's not safe."

I made my daughter stand up on her little feet. She placed both of them on my thighs and smiled at me, with her gray eyes. She had a dimple on each cheek. I kissed her on the forehead. "Yo, I told you about cursing in front of her. We gotta guard our tongues. Nah' mean? My baby precious." I mugged Rayven.

"Did you hear what I said, Kaleb? I think we should leave New York and go somewhere else. I mean, why are we even here to begin with? I mean, besides your mother and Derez?"

I scoffed and looked into my daughter's eyes. "I know you're a little nervous right now, but I ain't about to let nobody run me away from my homeland. New York is in my heart. Everywhere else sucks, if you ask me. Yo, we gon' find Buddy, and handle them Jamaican studs. It's only a matter of time before this war is over with, trust me on that." I picked my daughter up and made her fly over my head like Super Girl. A line of slob dropped on to my face, catching me off guard.

Rayven plopped down on the sofa next to me. "What if you wind up losing this war, Kaleb? Bullets ain't got no names on 'em. That's bad enough. But, it's ten times worst when bullets really do have names on 'em, and all of them are meant for you. Every time you walk out of that door, I am sick with worry. I can't eat. I can't sleep. I can't even think straight. I'm losing weight. I can't handle this shit." She covered her mouth after she let out the swear word. Looked me over closely.

I frowned and set my daughter on my lap. Wiped her slob from my face and kissed her. "Yo, I'm naming her Destiny after my sister. You can get the middle name. You cool wit that?"

Rayven shook her head and slammed her fist into the palm of her hand. "Yo, why are you ignoring me, kid? You about to have me all vexed in a minute. I'm trying to be cool." She said this, jumping from the couch, staring down at me.

I rubbed a tuft of Destiny's wavy hair, then kissed her small forehead again. As long as I had my daughter in my arms, it seemed like it was impossible for me to lose my cool. Her eyes closed, and within minutes, she fell asleep in my arms. I laid her in her crib and swaddled her in her Disney Princess blanket. Kissed her forehead and made my way back into the living room, where Rayven was sitting at the table, pouring herself another glass of wine. I grabbed the bottle and took a sip out of it. "Aiight, what's yo problem now, ma? My baby sleep. Everything is good. The floor is yours." I lowered myself to the couch, looking over at her.

"I want out of New York. I want us to take our daughter to the other side of the country. Start fresh and get into real estate over there. Maybe open a few businesses. I got a lot of money put up, and so do you. We can invest it, and see our cream add up. Ain't no sense of being in this run-down city warring with lowlifes when we have a daughter who needs us. I want out. Now, Kaleb! Things are way too dangerous. Please see it my way." I sat there with my head hung for a few minutes, thinking things over.

I knew she made a good point. We had enough money to flee to another city and buy up properties. Flip them and accrue even more income. I could cop a few restaurants and we could make money that way as well. I honestly didn't have to pick up another pack or flip another kilo of heroin if I didn't want to. I could go all the way legit and capitalize off of what I had been blessed with in the game so far. I wanted to be there for my daughter. Every step of the way. I knew she was going to need me, because the world was a cold place to be. It seemed like people were getting more and more cruel every single day. I would have to be around to protect her from the world.

But then, there was my mother and Derez, also Bree. They needed me as well. How could I leave them behind to go about my life? I had been there for them for as long as I could remember. I couldn't turn my back on them. It wasn't in me to. So, while some of things Rayven said made sense, it just felt like she wasn't seeing the bigger picture. "Rayven, what about my mother? What about Derez? Are they coming with us?"

She exhaled and shrugged her shoulders. "Yo, I don't know, Kaleb. Damn, we got a whole ass daughter now. When do we leave your baggage behind and focus on the baggage we have under our own roof? You can't keep trying to provide for and protect everybody. Sooner or later that stuff is going to take a toll on you. And by the way, you're going, it's going to take a toll on your life because you don't know how to go soft, you always gotta go so hard. Why can't it just be our little family? Why?"

I frowned and stood up. "Because it can't. I gotta make sure my mother and my little brother stay up top! All they got is me. If I don't put the food on the table, then they don't eat. My father was a bitch-ass nigga. He ran out on us before I could even piss straight. I'll never be like him. I'd rather die than to give up on my family or leave them to fend for themselves in New York. Only the stronger survive here, and I'm their muscle! Me! Just me!"

She shook her head. "But, you can't be their sacrifice for the rest of your life, Kaleb. Sooner or later, they are going to have to fend for themselves. You have a daughter now. I am your fiancée. You are about to be married. Damn! Nigga, you can't be a superhero to everybody. They will be alright."

12

"Yo, if you say that shit again, I'ma smack you in your mouth. Word up. My mom's sick right now. My little brother is still reeling over Destiny's death. On top of that, he's a target. Any one of them fools see kid anywhere in the Apple slipping, they gon' knock his head off. That's what war is. So, if you're planning on fleeing like some coward, then you gon' put them chips up so my moms and brother can flee too. I ain't leaving them behind. Not now, not never. Case muthafuckin' closed. You understand me?" I felt my blood pressure rising.

She waved me off. "You wilding. And I like how you can sling all these curse words at me, but you want us to speak lovely around Destiny. That's a double standard. How about you have some respect for the woman that pushed her out? I been feeling like shit ever since I did. No appreciation been coming from ya ass. None, kid. That shit starting to make me feel some type of way, adding to my post-partum and all of that shit. Word up." She turned her back to me. "Don't let me find out that all you wanted from me was a child, Kaleb. Yo, I swear I'll leave you two alone to be with each other. That's on my mother."

"You always gotta be so damn dramatic. Damn, that's so unattractive. Yo, I gotta get out of here for a second. My head is spinning too bad. You fucking me up, Rayven, as always."

"Yo, my word, I ain't start fucking you up until you started fucking Bree. After you came from between her thighs, you been acting real foul towards me, Kaleb. Yo, and it's breaking me down so bad. But I'm tired of crying. I'm tired of it. I'm to the point that I don't even care about being alone anymore. So, if you wanna run out of the door and go back to that bitch, then do it. Just go. I'm not even kidding." She walked to the door and opened it wide. I could see clear out to the street in front of the house.

A car rolled past, and a draft breezed into the house from outside. "Rayven, close the door before you let a draft in here and my baby get sick. Close the fucking door!" I snapped, rushed over and slammed it. Now Destiny was up and hollering at the top of her lungs. That irritated me even more. "Damn, it's always something with you. Don't you get tired of all of this arguing shit? That's why I don't like being around you for long periods of time. It's just exhausting. Fuck." I made my way to the room where Destiny was.

I picked her up out of the crib. She began to scream louder, until I bounced her up and down, patting her Pamper. "It's okay, mama. It's okay. Daddy right here. I ain't going nowhere. You got me, baby." I wiped tears from her little cheeks.

When I got back into the living room, Rayven was holding a thirty-eight Special in her hand. "All you care about is that baby, ain't it?" She put a bullet into the chamber and dropped the box on the floor. Bullets spilled out of it. She spun the chamber and snapped it in place. Cocked the hammer. I held Destiny by the back of her head and placed her face into my chest.

"Yo, what are you doing, Rayven?"

"You don't care about me, Kaleb, it's oh so clear. All you care about is our daughter. So, why am I here?" She put the gun to her temple and pulled the trigger.

Click!

She took it away and spun it again. Placed it back to her temple. I looked for someplace to put Destiny. Her mother was tripping. For as long as I had known her, I'd never known her to be suicidal or attempting anything like she was doing right there in front of me and our daughter. It was blowing my mind.

I rushed Destiny back into her bedroom and placed her in her crib. As soon as I set her down, she started to scream at the top of her lungs. But, I couldn't focus on that. I had to get back into the living room before Rayven killed herself. When I got back in there, I nearly had a heart attack.

T.J. Edwards

Chapter 2

There, smack dab in the middle of the living room stood Rayven, and on the side of her was Buddy. He had a shotgun pressed up against her lips, with three of his goons from New Orleans standing behind him with red rags around their necks, and mugs on their faces. I saw the hammers on the double-barrel shotgun were cocked back and ready to be fired. One of the dudes from Buddy's crew had a handful of Rayven's hair. Her head was pulled backward at an awkward angle. The gun she'd attempted to take her life with was on the floor right in front of her. The chamber on it was open and emptied of the lone bullet she'd loaded it with. Tears ran out of her eyes. There was a big smile on Buddy's face. I felt sick.

"Well, well, well. What it do, Blood?" he asked, laughing just a bit. He raised his arm, so the shotgun was leveled against her lips. I had a .40 Glock in the small of my back, and I had visions on grabbing it and firing until it was empty. I would never let this nigga harm my daughter or take me alive. Rayven appeared to be caught up in a sticky situation. One false move and all it would take would be for him to pull the trigger. He'd blow her head right off of her neck. I'd used a double-barrel shotgun on someone at close range before, it was sure to decapitate a person. I didn't want Rayven to suffer that fate. Even though, minutes earlier she was threatening to take her own life. I loved her and knew I had to protect her at all costs. I had to play things cool.

I took a step toward them and held my hands at shoulder level. "Yo, Buddy, she ain't got shit to do wit what you and I got going on, Blood. You can let her go and we can handle this shit ourselves. Nah' mean?"

He shook his head. "N'all, you see that's where you're wrong at, B. One you crossed me. Lied to the fam about that lil scratch and got my hand chopped off. Then, if that wasn't enough, yo trifling ass start fucking wit my baby mother behind my back. And, get the bitch pregnant. Nigga, this shit got everything to do wit this bitch right here. Since I can't find Bree, I'ma blow her shit off in her place. Then, I'ma kill that newborn bitch in that back room, before I whack yo punk ass. That's how this is going to go down. Word up," he snickered. "Unless you can convince me otherwise."

I could hear Destiny screaming at the top of her lungs. I was praying she quieted down. I wondered if I had cursed my daughter by naming her after her aunt that had received such a tragic fate. How was I going to protect her to make sure she wouldn't have to? I couldn't drop the ball twice. I shook my head. "I done took the rap for you for plenty shit growing up. Nigga, I got three slugs in me for some drama you kicked off. Drama I ain't have nothing to do wit. But, I took them slugs like a man, because I fucked wit you the long way. They could have ended my life, but I survived, nigga. I thought—"

"Nigga, cry me a muthafuckin' river. What the fuck that shit got to do wit what we're faced with right now? You fucked my bitch, got my hand cut off, and stabbed me in the back. Yo, you gone have to come better than them slugs you got in ya ass right now. I'm talking you got a matter of seconds." He looked over his shoulder. "Blood, one of y'all go back there and shut that bitch up. All that screaming and shit is getting on my nerves. Word up." He smiled at me.

One of his goons made their way toward me and the bedroom. I upped my .40 Glock and cocked that bitch. "On my mother, you finna have to kill me. Ain't neither one of you bitch niggas about to lay a hand on my seed. That's my word."

I tapped the trigger and enacted the red beam on top of the gun. Placed the dot right on Buddy's forehead. His eyes trailed upward until they crossed, tracing the beam. His boys jumped back, then upped their guns and aimed them at me. "Tell them bitch niggas to drop it, Buddy. Now! Nigga, my word, we all about to die in here," I hollered, and this made Destiny cry louder.

That made my eyes water. I had a feeling all of us were about to meet the Reaper and although I wasn't ready to go, there was no way I could stand back and let them hurt my child. They would be forced to do that over my dead body.

"Kaleb, you pussy-ass nigga. If you don't take that beam off of my head, nigga, I'm about to blow her shit back. And you know I ain't playing, either. If I'll kill my own daughter, you know I'll kill this punk bitch." He jugged the gun against her lips, causing them to bleed. I could hear her moaning and groaning.

"Fuck nigga, you do it, and I'ma blast you. They might blast me, but I'ma knock ya memories out of ya head for sure. That's my word." I slowly came closer to him but made sure my body stayed blocking the entrance to the hallway that led to my daughter's bedroom. I was ready for an all-out gunfight. I felt like my whole life had led up to this. You live by the sword, you die by the sword. It was what it was.

Rayven wiggled her head just enough to open her lips. "Please don't do this, Buddy. We'll pay you. We'll pay you to go away. Just name your price. Then, take the money and go. Please," she whimpered, and I didn't know if I completely agreed with her.

I didn't respect this nigga, especially after what he did to my sister and his daughter. I knew I could never bow down and tuck my tail. I wasn't about to pay him shit. I wanted to pull the trigger and knock his head off of his neck. What happened afterward just happened. I didn't even give a fuck no more, until I thought about my defenseless baby girl in the other room. Her screaming had stopped. Now she was crying just loud enough for me to hear her. "Bitch, how much money is you talking? Huh? That shit better be way up there too. I'm talking some serious figures," Buddy spat, with saliva flying out of his mouth.

"Whatever you want. Just name your price and I'll make it happen. I promise. Nobody has to die here tonight. There has been enough killing. Please let me squash this bullshit." I curled my lip and tightened my finger over the trigger. I was seconds away from pulling it. It was shaped like a hair trigger and I was ready to pull that bitch's hair. Word.

Buddy looked over at me and lowered his eyes. "Three million, bitch. I know y'all got it. I want three million in cash, or this shit gon' only get worse," he said through clenched teeth, mugging me the whole time. I took two steps backward toward the hallway. My daughter had gotten awfully quiet. I worried about her. I knew she was not past the Sudden Infant Death stage. She'd been crying and screaming so hard and loud, I worried she'd hurt herself in some way.

"Nigga, take that paper and get yo bitch ass on. It's either that or we all die here tonight. I'm letting you know right now I ain't going. I ain't giving you shit, and if you buss, I buss. I'm knocking yo shit off, and letting the cards fall where they might."

"Shut up, Kaleb. Damn. Before this crazy ass nigga kill me," Rayven cried. Her face was beet red. I could see her shaking from where I stood. I felt sorry for her. To see a nigga with a gun pressed to her face. I also pictured seeing my sister's body lying in her casket. The knife wounds all over her face, the big slice in her neck that looked like an open mouth. Next to her casket was Breeyonna's, the poor baby. He'd refused to spare either of the two.

My mind started to race, and I became angry. My heart began to pound in my chest like crazy. Sweat slid down my back and stopped at the waistline of my pants. My mouth and throat were both dry, as if I'd eaten a handful of baby powder.

"Aiight, let's go, Rayven. You gon' come wit me. You get me this money, and I'll go on about my bidness and forget you two ever existed. I'll even let that new bitch live," he snickered, and eyed me with hate in his eyes. "Let's go, Blood, this bitch coming wit us." He moved from behind her and pressed the shotgun to her temple.

One of his guys opened the front door and turned back to aim his gun at me. It took all of the restraint I had in me to not start bussing back to back. My mind flashed from my sister's funeral, then to the day of my daughter's birth. If I started shooting, I was sure to kill Buddy. That was a given. But then, he would pull his trigger and kill Rayven. One or two of his guys would hit me up, and I could die. Also, one of their bullets could fly through the wall and hit my baby girl. And even if that did not happen, after Buddy killed Rayven, I killed him and his guys killed me, Destiny would be without parents in a cold-ass world. She didn't stand a chance. I had to think logically and secure her first and for most. She was my seed. I couldn't be so stupid and callous. They slowly made their way out of the door with all eyes on me. Every time they took a step backward, I took a step forward, feeling like shit because I couldn't save my baby mother. That I was allowing the man that had killed my sister and goddaughter to walk out of my house untouched. I felt like a pussy. Like a simp. Weak. I couldn't believe myself.

"That's right, Kaleb. Just be smooth. We gon' take this bitch, get this money and everything gon' be all right. Feel me?" Buddy asked, with his eyes lowering. Rayven whimpered. Looked me in the eyes.

"Please, just let him take me, baby. It's okay. It's okay. I'll be back in a minute." Though these words came from her mouth, I was sure I would never hear from her again. I knew Buddy would kill her as soon as he got the money, and because of that I couldn't allow for that to happen. The man in me wouldn't allow it. I turned the beam, so it shined right into his left eye.

"Nall, nigga, let Rayven go. I don't trust yo punk ass. We'll drop the money off at a later time. But, let her go and tell yo niggas to drop they guns, right now."

"Kaleb, no! Please, baby! Just let him take me!" she screamed.

"What! Nigga, stop playin' wit me. This bitch coming wit us. When I get my money, I'll let her go. Y'all keep moving!" he ordered.

"Please, it's good, Kaleb. I'll be back. Please don't do nothin' stupid. I promise, I'll be back." I bit into my bottom lip so hard, I drew blood. I didn't know what to do. I was so confused. I watched them lead her to Buddy's Chevy Caprice and toss her inside, before they skirted down the street, Buddy laughing at the top of his lungs.

I ran into the street, with images of Rayven and me when we were kids playing at recess going through my mind. Suddenly, the tears came. I knew I would never see her again. I broke down, right there in the middle of the street. Stayed that way for what must have been ten minutes. Until Ajani's money green Porsche pulled up. He jumped out with three of his Camden hittas and surrounded me. All of them had guns in their hands.

Ajani knelt and placed his hand on my shoulder. "Lil cuz, what's good, Blood?" He looked around, then back down to me. I made my way to my feet, feeling sick on the stomach.

"That bitch nigga, Buddy, took Rayven. He hollering he want three million dollars. I know he about to kill my baby mother after she drop that bread, so we gotta find him first. I had my beam on that nigga head, son. I should have pulled the trigger, but he would have iced her."

Ajani blew air out of his jaws and swallowed. "Man, dawg, this shit don't get no easier," he said, running his big hand over his face. He shook his head and stopped in his tracks. I turned around to look at him. My body felt weak and drained of energy. I felt like I was missing something.

"What don't get no easier?" I asked, looking his hittas over carefully. They refused to make eye contact with me. Ajani took a deep breath and looked up at me. "Them dread heads clapped back, lil cuz. They snatched Derez and your mother and sent word that the only way you'd ever see either one again, is if you trade yourself, for both of them. The reason why I'm here right now is because I just got off of the phone with your mother. She say she sick and need her medication. I got it in the car, but I don't know which way to go. I'm sorry, kid."

I fell to my knees again. This time, I couldn't take it anymore. I broke the fuck down. It felt like all of my enemies were coming at me at once, hitting me from every angle. I felt trapped. Lost and confused. I cried so hard I got dizzy before I stood up to gather myself.

Ajani rubbed my back, with a mug on his face. "Yo, I got the drop on Damian. I had a few of my close ones check the move on his duck-off by the Delaware River. His headquarters is in 'The Alley', that's a drug infested spot over in New Jersey, right around Camden where my lil niggas from, and where we used to live. I know that hood like the back of my hand. My pops used to run that bitch before the Jamaicans took it over once he got indicted. Anyway, I'ma about to have the Ski Mask Cartel mount up and take that flight out this way, so we can go at these niggas head-on. I got you, Blood. I'll never leave you to fend for yourself. Let's get on some bloody shit. Word up," he said, frowning.

I strolled back into the house, thinking things over. At this point, I really didn't have a choice. Muthafuckas had backed me into a corner, where the only thing that made sense was murder, and lots of it. In a matter of weeks, I had lost my sister and my goddaughter. My baby mother got snatched, and now my enemies had taken my ill mother and baby brother. I ain't have shit to lose. I stopped in the living room and nodded to him. "It's on, nigga. These niggas think it's sweet, aiight then, let's give 'em cavities." I shook up with him and gave him a half-hug.

I walked in the direction of my daughter's room, after he turned his back and started to walk in the opposite direction. His guys stayed in the living room on security as if they had been trained properly by street savages. When I walked into the room, I felt a slight breeze. The window was wide open, causing the curtain to blow. I knew for a fact it had been shut. I made sure of that.

My heart dropped into my stomach. I slowly approached her crib afraid of what I was to find. I felt a sharp pain shoot through my chest. It hobbled me. I got dizzy and fell to my knees. My face hit the carpet. The room began to spin. I closed my eyes and whispered her name, "Destiny." I remembered how it had felt to hold her in my arms for the first time. Then everything faded to black.

Chapter 3
Three days later...

Bomp. Bomp. Bomp. "Nigga, open dis got damn doe," Ajani yelled, beating on the door. "You been in dat mafuckin' room for three days straight. It's time you get yo ass out here, and we go handle dis bidness," he hollered through the bedroom door from the hallway.

I was fucked up. I felt numb. I struggled to get up from the side of the bed. There was still traces of China White residue on my upper lip. I'd spent the last three days binging on heroin, tooting one gram after the next until my nostrils were raw on the inside. After I found out my daughter had been kidnapped through her bedroom window, I lost it. Mentally, I was unable to think logically. My brain felt like it had shut down completely. There had been no word from Buddy, or Rayven. I didn't know if Derez and my mother were still alive either. Damien had called off the meeting he and I was supposed to have. He sent word through his killas that he would summon for me when the time was right. He'd also said when he called for me, I was to come and grace his presence with a financial gift that would right the wrongs that both Buddy, and myself had caused his Jamaican people. I didn't know what he meant by that shit and I didn't give a fuck what he was talking about. Especially since he was saying that no matter how much money I brought him that I should be ready to trade in my life in exchange for those of my brother, and mother. I still didn't know which of the two had my daughter. Buddy wasn't answering his phone, and Damien wasn't going to utter another word to me outside of the message that he had already sent through his killas. So yeah, with all of this shit heavy on my brain, the only escape I could come up with was that dog food, and it was fuckin me up. My ears stared to ring. I laid on my back, scratching the right side of my neck. It felt like a million bugs were crawling on me there.

Bomp. Bomp. Bomp. Bomp. Ajani beat on the door harder. "Say Joe, if you don't open dis ma'fucka in the next three seconds I'm bout to kick dis bitch in," he threatened.

I groaned and stretched out on the floor, stayed there for a minute, before I slowly made my way to my knees. I used the bed to help me to climb to my feet. I stood up. The world felt like it was spinning all around me. I staggered to the door and opened it. I was high as a cloud and numb as Novocain.

Ajani pushed the door inward. "Joe, you in dis ma'fucka acting soft as a bitch. How da fuck we finna find dese niggas if you in here nodding in and out off dat dope and acting all down on yo self?" he asked, mugging me.

I ran my hand over my face and squeezed my eyelids as tight as I could. "Yo kid, lower yo fuckin voice. You ain't talking to one of dem worker ass niggas out there. Dis Kaleb, B." I opened my eyes and looked him over like he'd lost his fuckin mind.

Ajani was caramel-skinned with brown eyes. He was about five feet eight inches tall, real muscular with a temper as lethal as mine. He was my cousin, and had come all the way from Chicago, Illinois to assist me out here in New York. Out of all of my family, I loved him and my cousin Rayjon the most. They were brothers. Their hearts were as cold as ice. They murdered with no remorse and like me, they were crazy about our family, and about obtaining duffel bags of cash. My bloodline was bananas.

"Nigga, fuck what you talking about. It's time to get on bidness. We finna go at dat nigga Damien chin. I told you, I got the whole run-down on his whole operation. I say we start pulling kick does and knocking his people off one by one. Fuck dem dread heads, nigga. I ain't scared to go up against they ass." He clenched his teeth. I could see the muscles in his jaw flexing.

"Cuz, you been in the streets for the last three days. Yo, tell me you heard something about Destiny. I'm bout to flip my lid, son. Word up."

Ajani lowered his head. "N'all B., ma'fuckas ain't got word on yo daughter yet. Dat's why I say we start fuckin niggas over so we can get some answers. Dawg, the longer we sit back and do nothing, the more shit gon get out of hand. Let's go at these niggas' chins. Fuck is we waiting on?"

I nodded. I felt sick that there were no new developments when it came to my baby. I was missing my daughter like crazy. She wasn't even a year old, and already she was reaping the pains of my sins. That shit had me feeling lower than a sewer. "Say, Dunn, let me get myself together. I need to shower and some other shit. Den when I get fresh, I'ma be ready to hit up da slums and get to it."

Ajani looked me up and down from the corners of his eyes. "Yeah, aiight, nigga. Dat shit sound slick. Before you do all dat doe, I got a couple niggas in here I want you to meet." He waved for me to follow him.

I followed him into the living room where he had two dudes tied to metal chairs. He had duct tape around their mouths, eyes, wrists and ankles. One had long dreads that fell to the carpet. He had on a white tee shirt that was drenched in blood. The blood dripped from his nose. He groaned under the duct tape. The other had short nappy dreads. He was heavyset, and equally as fucked up physically as the other man. Behind them were two of Ajani's savages. They held double-barrel shotguns to the back of each man's head.

Ajani stood in front of the man with the long dreads. He smacked his face as hard as he could, then looked over to me. "You see dis bitch nigga? Dis nigga fuck with Damien and dem Camden County Boys real tough. Word from my snipers is dat he move at least three traps under Damien." Ajani smacked his face again. This time he hit him so hard, he almost knocked him out of the chair. The sound of the slap resonated through the house. Then Ajani pulled the duct tape from his mouth.

The captive coughed and spit on my carpet. A rope of blood leaked from his mouth onto the carpet. It looked like a red shoestring. He smacked his swollen lips and got ready to say something.

Ajani grabbed him by the throat and dug his nails into his flesh. "Bitch nigga, where the fuck Damien keeping my auntie and my lil cousin?" He released his throat.

The captive let out a gust of air. "Fuck mon, ma don't know. Haven't seen't or heard no-ting bout ya people. Ya got da wrong guy, rude boy."

"What? One of you bitch niggas know something. Bam! *Bam*! *Bam*! Ajani punched him three hard times in the mouth, busting through his teeth. His fist disappeared inside of his mouth, before he pulled it out and kicked him in the chest as hard as he could. The chair flew backward. Before it even hit the ground, Ajani was on top of him. He pulled a .45 from the small of his back and turned the gun around so the handle was out. He raised the gun in the air and proceeded to beat the Jamaican over the head with it over, and over again. I could see the handle planting holes in the man's forehead. Blood popped up and splashed the walls. When Ajani that he had made a big enough statement, he stood up and looked down on the Jamaican. "Ma'fuckas ain't got no time to be playin' dese games. Where my people at?"

The Jamaican winced in obvious pain. The binds didn't allow for him to move much. There were eight big holes in his forehead. Blood oozed out of them like fruit punch. His eyelids were squeezed tightly together. He looked as if he were seconds from passing away.

"Ma'fucka, say somethin! Now!" Ajani hollered.

The Jamaican kicked his legs. He laid out flat as he could with the chair attached to him. He shook like crazy. Blood continued to ooze from his wounds. Then he stopped moving altogether.

Ajani walked over and kicked him in the rib cage. "Say nigga? Wake yo ass up. I'm talking to you."

I stepped in front of the heavyset Jamaican mugging him. His cold gray eyes looked into mine. Sweat peppered the side of his face. I ripped the duct tape off of his mouth and flung it to the ground. "Where the fuck me people at, Dunn?"

He shook his head. "Ma don't know wat you talking 'bout. Ya barking up da wrong tree, doe. Damien catch wind and he gon gut ya like a fish, ya bumbaclot."

Ajani stood up and stepped beside me. "Fuck he just say?" He made a move to go at him.

I stopped him by sticking my arm out. "Nah son, kid belong to me." I looked the heavyset Jamaican over from the corners of my eyes. "Yo, I understand you ain't got shit to do wit what happened to my people and all dat good shit. But you finna have to tell me something. Where da fuck Damien live?"

The Jamaican looked at me like I was stupid. "Kill me rude boy. Me never snitch. I'm from Kingston. Honor over pain." He hawked a loogey and blew it right into my face. The spit slapped my cheek and exploded. It felt hot and thick. The smell was damn near unbearable.

Ajani jumped back and aimed his gun at him. "Aw, hell nall. Move out da way, I'm finna blow his shit back."

I took off my shirt, and wiped my face. I felt disgusted. I was heated. I felt me blood pressure rise to its highest levels. "Yo, hand me that pole, kid."

Ajani handed me his pistol, and stepped back. "Blow dat nigga, cuz. Dat bitch nigga spit in yo face. Aw, hell nall. Dat's death. Smoke him."

"So you gon spit in my shit, and you ain't gon tell me where my people at? Aiight." I spun the gun around after making sure that it was on safety. Then I was beating him over the forehead repeatedly like a maniac, faster and harder. I could feel his bone ricocheting off of the steel of the gun. His blood popped everywhere just like his homies' had, and I kept on beating him senseless until my arm gave out. I staggered backwards and stood up.

Ajani placed his fist in front of his mouth. "Hell yeah. Dat's how a ma'fucka supposed to look when you get on day ass. Look how his shit oozing out of him. Whew! Dat's a pretty sight." He smiled.

I stood looking down on him, my chest heaving up and down. My vision was hazy at first. Now it was coming back to normal. I handed Ajani his gun back. It was dripping with blood. "Huh, cuz."

He took it and wiped it on the Jamaican's face. Then he placed it into the small of his back. He kept smiling at the sight of the fallen man as if he were impressed with what I had done.

"Dawg, we gotta get rid of dese niggas. Den we gotta get out there and find my daughter, Derez, my mother, and Rayven. Dem punk ass Jamaicans seem like they a lost cause. They ain't 'bout that snitching shit at all, kid."

"Bullshit. We just gotta get some better tools. Them ma'fuckas used to being tortured. They come from the slums of Kingston, Joe. Ma'fuckas been handling dem rough since the beginning of time. Dat's what we gotta do. Don't trip though, I'm on dat."

I nodded in agreement. "I gotta find dis nigga Buddy too. Something telling me he got my daughter. If he'll kill his own seed, you already know what he'll do to mine."

"Dat's if he ain't already done it yet." Ajani said.

That sent a cold chill down my spine. "Don't say dat shit, cuz. Damn, don't say dat." I felt like I was ready to panic. I missed my daughter. I had barely even gotten chance to get to know Destiny. That fact was making me sicker and sicker on the stomach. First I had failed my little sister Destiny, and I'd thought that I could keep her memory alive by naming my newborn baby girl after her, but it seemed that all I'd done was curse her with the plague of death. "Yo, I'ma regroup, then we finna hit up Brooklyn, Harlem, The Bronx, and turn New Jersey upside down if we have too. I'm done accepting this shit without doing nothing. I need to check on Bree, and we'll go from there."

"Well, you do what you gotta do. I'm finna get some pussy and regroup. Pussy always get my head back in the game. We'll meet back up in a few days. If I find somethin out before then. I'ma be at you. Know that, cuz." He gave me a half-hug and signaled for his troops to get rid of the bodies.

I felt lost for a second. Frozen in place. I couldn't understand how my entire life had spiraled out of control so swiftly? I felt like the Devil was playing a sick joke on me. A joke I refused to take part in. I felt targeted and under the gun. I knew I had to get on some murderous shit if I had any chance of seeing my family ever again. I nodded my head, getting geeked up. I felt my heart turning colder and colder. I knew what I had to do. After I confirmed Bree was good, I was about to get on bidness. I didn't have any other choice.

T.J. Edwards

Chapter 4

"I can't believe dis shit is happening to us, Kaleb. It's only so much a person can take," Bree whimpered. She wiped her tears away with a hand towel. Her nose was red from blowing it so much. She looked like she had lost a few pounds. Though it did very little to take away from her thick body structure. Even though Bree was in mourning, she was still bad. She ran her fingers through her naturally curly hair and looked over to me. I lowered my face to the four lines of China I had separated for us. I took one line halfway up my right nostril, then finished it with my left. I pinched my nose and sat back on the couch. I could hear music playing in my head. My entire body felt like I was floating. "Shorty, I know we can't bring back Breeyonna Destiny, but it'll kill us if we sit around mourning, every second of every day. We gotta move past the loss of them. I know it's gone be damn near impossible to do, but we have to. We need to get out there and find out where Buddy is roaming. Then me and my cousin gotta go at these Jamaicans because it's clear that they're out for blood as well. I don't know when Buddy, or the Jamaicans are going to try and strike again. But I know sooner or later that you are going to be a target. If anything ever happened to you, Bree, I would never be able to live with myself. You understand me."

She nodded. She got down to her knees and knelt in front of the raw on the table. She picked up a pink straw and tooted half the line. Coughed. Then finished it with her other nostril. Her eyes were closed tight. She rubbed her nose. "I don't like doing dis shit, Kaleb. I don't like putting dis shit in my body, but it's the only thing that takes the pain away. I need it." She stood up and stepped in front of me.

I looked up and down her thick frame. She was wearing a pair of red, lace boy shorts that were all up in her crease. Her thick thighs appeared to be freshly oiled. Her tank top was tight. It made her breasts look so good to me. The bumps of her nipples poked at the fabric. "Shawty, come mere once."

She stepped forward again. "What's good?"

I took my hand and rubbed all over her plump lips through her boy shorts. It took less than thirty seconds before she was moaning deep within her throat. Her shorts grew damp. She spaced her feet. "Feel good, baby?"

She bit on her bottom lip and nodded. Her curls bounced. "Yeah, daddy, it do."

I palmed her ass cheeks and pulled her to me. My nose rested right on her front. I sniffed her box, then kissed all over her camel toe. "I'm stressing, baby. I need some of dis pussy. You hear me?" Now my tongue was licking all over her front.

"Yes. Mmm. Daddy. Yes." She placed her pedicured right foot on the couch and pulled her material to the side. Her dark caramel pussy lips popped out. They were juicy, with a hint of dew on them. Her scent was heavier than usual, as if it had been about a day since she'd showered.

I worked my tongue into her hole, while I held her juicy lips apart. She bucked into my face. Her wet pussy smeared across my cheeks. I gripped that fat ass harder.

"Mmm. Mmm. Daddy. We not supposed to be... Uhhhh! Shit daddy." She balanced herself by holding onto my shoulders. Her ass jiggled while she humped my face as if she was fucking it. Her juices tasted extra salty, with a hint of sweetness. Her clitoris stood up like a pinky finger. I wrapped my lips around it and sucked harder.

She screamed and came, pulling on the back of my head so that my face was all in between her legs. Her meaty lips seemed to be wrestling with the lips attached to my face.

I stood up and picked her lil ass up, before sitting her on the couch. I spread her thick thighs wide and placed her ankles on my shoulders. "Baby, I know we going through something. I know we fucked up right now, but just let daddy heal you the best way he know how. Okay?"

She opened her thighs wider. "Okay daddy. Go ahead."

I spread her lips with my thumbs and exposed her pink. It looked glossy. Her brown rosebud winked at me. My tongue explored her hungrily. I sucked each lip, licked around her pearl, before tugging on it with my lips. This made her scream again. Then she was riding my face from her back on the couch. Her ankles forced my head deep into her groove. Her nails dug into my shoulders. My tongue went into overdrive. I fucked in and out of her at full speed. Her cream dripped off of my chin and drove me crazy. I slumped into her cat and trapped her clit again.

"Daddddeeeeee!" she screamed. She bucked into my face harder, and harder before cumming for the third time.

When I took my face away her juices were running down my neck on to my collarbone. I stood up, running my tongue all over my lips so I could taste her some more. "My turn, shorty." I already had my piece out of my Gucci jeans. I stroked him and felt it beating in my hand.

Bree grabbed him and came to her knees. She kissed the head and wet her thick lips. She stroked him up and down. "I need you, daddy. I need you to heal me. I'm so tired of going through this pain." She kissed the head again, then ran her tongue all around it, before sucking me into her mouth. Her jabs were short at first. Then gradually, she started to take in more, more of me.

My nose curled. I grabbed a handful of her hair and used her for leverage. Fuckin her mouth good. She pressed her lips together and sucked harder. I whimpered and grew weak in the knees.

She popped me out, still stroking. "Daddy, sit down. Let me handle dis bidness for you."

I followed her directives. I sat on the couch. She crawled between my legs and took ahold of my pipe again. She brought her tongue from my sack, all the way up to my head, and sucked me back into her mouth. In a matter of seconds, she was sucking at full speed. Her head speared into my lap over and over again. The sounds that emitted from her lips and my dick were driving me up the wall. She added plenty spit. The more she added, the faster she sucked.

I clawed at the arm of the chair, humping upward. I closed my eyes for a second because the pleasure was so intense. When I opened them, I saw how her nipples were poking through her tank top, and I couldn't hold back any longer. I came, groaning like I'd been shot or something.

Bree continued to suck. She pumped her fist up and down, swallowing my seed. When she felt like there was no more to be found, she squeezed me in her fist and slowly brought it from the base, all the way to the top. A drop of white gel appeared. She licked it off hungrily. She slowly stroked me. My dick was rock-hard, throbbing in her small fist. "Daddy, you gotta fuck me. It's been too long. I need this dick. Word up." She licked it up and down, before standing up.

I sat back on the couch with my shit jumping like crazy. "Get yo thick ass up here den, Shorty. Bounce on dis ma'fucka. Hurry up."

She stood before me, rubbing up and down her pussy. She opened the lips for me to see her candy, then she straddled my thighs. She took ahold of me, and slowly guided me inside of herself. Her eyes closed, before they did I could see they were rolling backwards. "Unnnn." She shivered as I filled her up. She sat on my balls.

I held her ass. "Bitch, fuck you waiting on? Ride daddy."
I lifted her up by her ass and slammed her down by her hips.

"Uh! Daddy. Mmm. Okay." She held the back of the
couch, then her thick ass was riding me nice and slow building
momentum.

I sucked all over her neck. Ripped her tank top from her
frame on some savage shit, and smushed her titties together.
My teeth pulled on her nipples, before I sucked them aggres-
sively. They swelled and stood up, longer and longer.

Bree got to riding me so fast that the couch was moving
further and further backward. Finally, it remained planted
against the wall. Tapping against it while she increased her
speeds. "Daddy. Daddy. Daddy. Uhhhh! Yes! Yes! Fuck!"
Faster and faster she rode, bouncing up and down with her
head thrown backward. Her nipples jutted from her breasts
like dark brown candy corns. "Uhhhh! Daddy, I'm cumming.
Aw fuck. I'm cummmmiiiing!" she screamed.

I bounced her up and down faster and harder. My piece
stretched as far into her as it could go. I pulled her to me, and
bit into her neck, cumming back to back.

Somehow, we fell to the floor, with her on her back and
her left ankle resting on the couch while I pounded her out
with no mercy. She dug her nails into my waist, begging me
to slow down. But I refused. The pussy was too good. I had to
cum in her guts again. I needed to heal myself I side of her.
So, I fucked her harder and harder until I couldn't hold back.
I blew deep within her belly, while sucking on her neck, and
holding her thigh against my shoulder.

***

After we climbed out of the tub, Bree climbed up my body.
She rubbed my chest and wrapped her left thigh across my

waist. She snuggled up against me. Her face was in the crux of my neck. "Daddy, I wanna get in dat field with you."

I rubbed all over her naked ass. It felt soft and hot. "Ma, what you talking about?" My fingers crept through her ass crack and wound up on her pussy lips again. My piece slipped inside of her. She was way too thick for me not to play in dat pussy every chance I got.

"Mmm." She kissed my neck. "Daddy, right now I am struggling to find a reason to breathe every day. When Buddy killed my daughter and we lost our baby, it took a lot out of me. I feel my heart is colder than it had ever been. The only way I can begin to find myself is if I turn into an animal like you. Although I think I already am." She kissed my neck again. "I'm ready to make ma'fuckas pay for what happened to Breeyonna."

I pulled her up closer to me. "So, you think you ready to get on that murder shit wit me? Huh? You ready to die, boo?"

She nodded. "Hell yeah. We living on borrowed time anyway. I already know that the Lord ain't hearing my prayers. If He was, none of this shit would've ever happened to my baby. It would've never happened to your sister either."

"I don't think that none of dis shit got anything to do with Jehovah. It's just the way life goes. You already know how I bet down. I take lives. Karma is a bitch. Sooner or later that shit had to come back on me. It just that it came back in a way that I would've never imagined. But it is what it is though. Ma'fuckas finna feel dis wrath, shorty. Know dat."

"Fuck karma, Kaleb. My daughter ain't never did nothing to karma. Karma should've never taken her away from me. Buddy is just the devil. I should've never been fuckin with him to begin with. I should've known that one of these days he was going to hurt me in a way I would never recover." She straddled me. "Baby, when it time to kill his ass you gotta let me do it. Please. That's all I ask of you. Please let me be the one to put a fucking bullet in his head. You and him, both of y'all owe me that."

I hugged Bree to me. I saw her eyes were starting to mist up again. I didn't want to see her cry any longer from some shit that Buddy had done to us. I smacked her lightly on the ass. "Get up, Bree."

"What?" She looked confused. "Daddy, what did I say?"

I slapped her ass harder. "Bitch, get up."

She climbed off of me and stood on the side of the bed. "What's the matter?"

I got up and walked over to the dresser. I grabbed a .45 automatic out of it and cocked it. Stepped to her and placed the barrel to her forehead, cocked the hammer.

Bree froze. "Daddy, I'm sorry. Please, whatever I did, I'm sorry."

"Man, fuck that." I pressed the barrel harder into her skin. "I'm tired of you doing all dis ma'fuckin' crying like you soft or something. From now on, every time you shed a mutha-fuckin tear, I'ma spank yo ass. You can't be soft. Dat shit ain't allowed. So you can take all dem ma'fuckin' tears and cry on yo own time, you understand me?"

Bree mugged me. "But you know why I keep crying, right?"

"I do, but it ain't no room for that shit, so stop it. Fuck that emotional shit. Dat punk took our blood away from us, and all we doing is sitting back wallowing like a bunch of pussies. Fuck that. You wanna shed tears you shed yo years through other people's eyes. Make dem ma'fuckas feel yo pain by use of dis bitch right here." I pushed against her forehead with the gun. "You understand me?"

She nodded. "Yeah, nigga, I do." She smacked the gun away from her face. Then she rushed me and wrapped her arms around my neck. "Let me buss dat gun for us, Kaleb. I know where all of Buddy's people are. Somebody gotta know where he is keeping Rayven, and maybe even your daughter if he got her. Let's hunt his ass down. I need to get my first kill after that, I'ma be good to go."

"After dat first kill, you gon be feening to settle yo debts by use of that sword. You gon see." I kissed her on the forehead. "Aiight den, li'l mama, dis what we on den. First thang in the morning we at that nigga, Buddy. For now, get yo strapped ass in the bed so I can feel dat ass in my lap." I smacked that big ma'fucka.

She smiled and climbed in the bed with her fat pussy present under her ass cheeks. She crawled halfway on the bed and looked back at me. "You gon be surprised how much killa I actually got inside of me. I am a reflection of you. Just watch."

I climbed in the bed next to her. "We'll see about that. For now, rest your mind, and just let daddy hold you."

She got comfortable against me. "Daddy, are you really gon spank me anytime I cry?"

"You muthafuckin right. Ain't no room for dat shit in the field. We make other muthafuckas cry. Now ourselves. So dat's over wit."

Okay, daddy. Just hold me. Tomorrow we at Buddy chin like an ingrown hair. "

Chapter 5

Bree rang the doorbell to Buddy's Aunt Toni's house and popped back on her legs. She looked over to me. "Daddy, dis nigga obsessed with his auntie Toni. Trust me when I tell you dat. If it's anybody that knows where Buddy is, it's her," she assured me.

I nodded and scanned the neighborhood. We were on the east side of The Bronx, and in foreign territory. I didn't know nothin about the niggas over dis way. Most of them for as far as I could see were Spanish. It was nine o'clock at night, and the street was slightly packed with Latinos. There were four trucks parked on the other side of the street from Toni's house. Their doors were open, and they were banging Reggaeton. On the sidewalk were about ten dudes nodding their heads and jamming to the music. I could smell the weed smoke they were puffing on. More than a few of them glanced our way as we waited for Toni to answer the door. I felt uncomfortable standing on the porch to her duplex.

Bree beat on the door again and tried the doorbell. It was broken. She tapped on the window and looked upwards toward the windows up that way. "Damn, I just got off of the phone with dis bitch. I wonder what's really good?"

I shrugged my shoulders and adjusted the .40 Glock tucked inside of my waistband. "I don't know what's really good, but I got a bad feeling about dis hood." I looked across the street again. Majority of the dudes over that way were mugging me with hatred it seemed. I got ready to start blowing at them if I had too. I knew that most Bronx niggas were shiesty, and real territorial. They probably started to see me as a threat or a victim since Toni wasn't answering the door. Four of them huddled up and kept looking across the street while they discussed something.

Bree peeped that shit. "Why dem Latin ma'fuckas keep looking over here like they on something?" she asked, with her nose turned up. She had a .380 in her purse, and she adjusted it so that it was close to her dominant left hand.

"I don't know, shorty, but if they come across that street, we just gon start bussing at they ass. You remember how to pop yo shit off safety?"

"Sho do. I'm wit you, daddy. You blow at them and I'm blowing until my shit empty. Word to Jehovah."

That response gave me chills. Bree seemed like she was turning into a killa and that was a complete turn-on for me. "Yo, somebody just moved dem curtains." I pointed at Toni's front window.

"Fa real?" Bree rubber necked to see what was good.

Finally, the door opened. Toni, Buddy's auntie, stood before us in a robe. I caught a whiff of sex and alcohol right away. I guessed that she had been getting her groove on. She looked from me to Bree and smiled. "Girl, I know you said you was on your way, but I didn't know you was gone show up dis fast," she said, placing her hand on her hip. Toni was five feet even, dark-skinned, and very shapely, with a bit of a gut that complemented her frame. She had chubby cheeks, and short hair. To me she was a beautiful older woman.

"Well, I told you I was in the area. You gon keep us on the porch all day long, or you gon let us in?" Bree asked, looking her over with a smile.

I was mugging the niggas across the street. They were watching us way too close. My Range Rover was parked right in front of Toni's house. I started to get nervous about leaving it there. "Toni, who is dem fuck niggas across the street?"

She looked past me. "Kaleb, you don't want no parts of dem. Dem boys always shooting at somebody. They just moved from the south side of The Bronx a few months back.

It's been chaos over here ever since den. Y'all come on in the house. They already looking over here and shit." She stepped to the side so we could get past her.

Bree walked into the house first. "Dang, girl, it smell rank in here."

I backed into the house looking dem niggas across the street over. I was praying I didn't have to blow at them boys before we left Toni's house. I'd brought one extra clip just in case, and made sure Bree had an extra clip on her as well. We didn't know what we were set to encounter at Toni's, but I wanted to make sure that we were prepared for everything.

Toni locked the door behind me. She laughed. "Girl, you act like you ain't never smelled a lil love making before. Me and my guy friend been at it all night, if you just must know. Dang, but he need a li'l breather, so I got time to pick of wit y'all for a minute." She turned to me. "Wow, Kaleb, so I don't get no hits from you no more?" She held open her arms. Her robe became undone enough for me to see the slopes of her breasts, all the way to her areoles.

I slid in and hugged her. Ran my hands over that big ass, cuffing the cheeks. I had never done nothing like that before, but I figured why not. That Molly had me rolling, and I'd mixed it with a few Percocets. I didn't give a fuck how she felt about what I was doing.

She tensed up and laughed. Then she wiggled out of my embrace. "Boy, I just told you that my guy friend was upstairs. What you trying to do get me in trouble or something?"

I shook my head and walked into the living room. "Fuck dude."

Bree followed me into the living room with an angry look on her face. I knew it was probably cause she'd watched me grab Toni's ass, but I didn't give a fuck. I had a thing for older women and like I said before, to me, Toni was gorgeous, and strapped. Bree sat beside me.

Toni sat across from us in the love seat. She crossed her thick thighs and caused the robe to fall back just a bit. "So, to what do I owe dis visit?" she asked, sipping from a glass of brandy she'd picked up from the table.

"I'ma cut straight to the chase. We need to know where Buddy is," I said.

Toni smiled. "Boy, you mean to tell to tell me that y'all came all the way over here for that? She could've asked me this shit on the phone."

"Well, I didn't, but we asking you now. So, where is Buddy staying right now?" Bree asked, with a cut to her voice. I could tell she was irritated.

Toni jerked her head backward. "Girl, who da fuck you talking to like that? You got me all the way fucked up."

"Is that right?" Bree scooted to the edge of the couch. "Toni, we ain't gon ask you again," she warned.

Toni laughed. "I'm supposed to be scared or something? What lil 'ol Bree done finally got herself some courage because she fuckin with her baby daddy's right-hand man behind his back?" She smacked her lips. "Bitch please. Matter fact, get yo slutty ass up and get out of my house. Right now." Toni stood up.

Bree remained seated. She looked at the carpet as if she were lost in a trance. "I remember the time Buddy busted my head right here in dis living room. You stood in the same spot that you're standing in right now, watching him kick my ass like it was the most natural thing in the world."

"A bitch get out of line, she gets taken care of. That's the way of the world. You had to do somethin for my nephew to go upside yo head. Just like he gonna have to do if he keep fuckin wit you."

44

"His steak was medium rare instead of well-done," Bree whispered.

"What, bitch?" Toni snapped. "Speak up, can't nobody hear yo crybaby ass.

Bree's looked up and trained her eyes on Toni. "I said, I'd made a mistake and cooked his steak medium rare instead of well-done. Because I had, he beat me right where that glass table is now, in front of our daughter."

Toni shrugged her shoulders. "And, what the fuck that got to do with me?"

Toni's heavyset boyfriend stepped into the living room with his shirt off. He scratched his beer belly. "Baby, what's all dis ruckus down here? A ma'fucka upstairs tryna to get some sleep."

I stood up and shook his hand. "What's good Blood, my name Kaleb. Toni like my auntie. And dat's my baby right there." I nodded my head toward Bree.

"Nice to meet you. I'm David. Hey lil lady, what's yo name?"

Bree ignored him. She stood up and stepped into Toni's face. "Toni, where is Buddy?"

Toni backed up. "Lil girl, you betta get yo ass put my face. I don't know what the fuck you thank dis is, but dis ain't..."

SLAP!

Bree slapped her so hard, she fell on to the couch holding her face. "Bitch, I ain't got time to be playin wit you. "Now where the fuck is Buddy?"

"I know dis lil bitch didn't just hit my woman." He made a move to pursue Bree.

I slid behind him and grabbed him by the throat, squeezing hard. "Dis shit ain't got nothin to do wit you homie. But see now you just involved yourself." I squeezed tighter while he slapped at my arm. He tried to pull it off of him, but I had his ass in a death lock.

Bree pulled out her gun. "Bitch, if you don't tell me where Buddy is, I am going to kill you. I'ma drop yo body in the same spot that he dropped mine that day," she said, with her eyes bucked.

Toni held up her hands. "I don't know, baby. Buddy don't tell me where he be at no more. He just pop up, and then he be gone again. I don't know what all he did to you, but please don't hold that shit against me. That's between y'all."

Bree shook her head. "You're lying. I know you stay in contact with him. You're the only one that he really trusts. So I'ma ask you again. Where is Buddy?"

David continued to squirm. I flipped his ass to the floor and placed my Timbs on his neck. "Nigga, if you keep moving, I'm finna pop yo ass. Now stay still."

"Man, y'all ain't got no beef with me. Dat's between her and Buddy. Let me go. I ain't gon say shit. I promise, man," he whimpered.

I hated when a nigga whimpered like a bitch. For some reason, that was just a trigger for my temper. I raised my foot as high as I could and slammed it on his neck. He made a choking sound. He jumped up, holding his throat, struggling to breathe.

"Get the fuck back down," I ordered.

He shook his head still holding his throat. He wheezed and fell to his knees. "Please, man? I'm beggin' you."

One kick to the chest sent him flying backward. I aimed the Glock down at him. "Nigga don't say shit else until she tell us what we wanna know. You got that?"

He nodded, still wheezing. Sweat was all over his chubby face. His eyes were blood shot red. He breathed with his mouth wide open.

"Why are y'all doing this, Kaleb? Why are y'all treating me like the enemy?" Toni hollered.

Bree cocked the hammer on her gun. "Bitch, where is Buddy?"

Toni was crying now. She shook like a leaf. "Harlem. He staying out in Harlem with some nigga named Zeke. Dat's all I know. I don't know what brownstone, or the address. That's all I got for you."

"Call him," Bree demanded.

"What?" Toni whimpered.

"Daddy, how do I pop dis gun and still keep it so that can't nobody outside hear what I'm doing?" Bree asked, with a smile on her face.

"Shorty, you see that throw pillow on the couch?" I asked.

"Yeah, I see it." Bree looked over to the couch.

"Grab one of dem ma'fuckas and put it on the barrel. Then blow at that bitch. She don't think that fat meat is greasy."

Bree grabbed the pillow off of the couch. I thought she was going to continue to threaten and question Toni, but she did none of that. She placed the pillow over the barrel of the gun and fired a shot. *Boof*!

Toni jumped up screaming as the bullet knocked a chunk out of her thigh. The hole began to seep with her blood. She hopped up and down on one leg, before falling back against the wall. I laughed, the beats of my heart sped up. I wanted to fuck the shit out of Bree for bussing her gun.

"Bitch, I ain't finna keep playing with you." The smell of burnt pillow was heavy in the air. She stood over Toni with a menacing look on her face. "Now, where the fuck is Buddy?"

Toni scooted as far back as she could. Tears ran down her face. "I swear, I don't know exactly. I just know he fuckin with Zeke and they out in Harlem. Past a hundred and thirty fifth and Lennox."

Bree stepped forward. "Call dat nigga and ask him where he is right now."

Toni shook her head. "Dat's my nephew. I don't want you hurting my baby."

"Oh really." Bree placed the pillow back to the barrel of the gun and let off two shots. Big holes appeared in Toni's legs again. Now she was wailing in pain. She dragged herself across the floor with her elbows. "Help me, Kaleb. Please baby. Please save me from this crazy bitch."

David squirmed under my feet. I didn't give a fuck no more. I aimed and fired two loud shots to the side of his cranium. His noodles splashed into the carpet. He'd jerked twice before laying still.

Now Toni was screaming like a maniac. She must've been sure we were there to kill her and Buddy. "Help me. Please Father, help me." She continued to crawl across the floor.

Bree followed her into the hallway. "Bitch, you think I got any sympathy for you? Dat nigga Buddy killed Breeyonna, and you are choosing to save him? Like you owe him any loyalty for killing a baby?" *Boof*! Another bullet punched a hole into Toni's right shoulder blade.

She hollered again. She continued to crawl. "He didn't mean to. He told you that he didn't mean to. He was just mad at you."

"What? That makes no sense." Bree walked alongside of her. "Toni, if you don't call Buddy, I am going to kill you."

Toni crawled to the kitchen and stopped. She curled into a ball. Her eyes were low. She appeared drowsy. I imagined the blood loss was starting to affect her. "I can't, baby. Buddy is my nephew. Besides I don't ever call him. He calls me from a restricted number."

Bree shook her head. "Stop lying! He killed my baby, and all you you're doing is protecting him. It's not fair. She was just a little girl!" *Boof*! *Boof*! *Boof*! *Boof*! *Boof*! *Click*! *Click*! *Click*! Bree dropped the gun and fell to her knees in tears.

I knelt beside her and wrapped my arm around her shoulder. "Fuck her, baby. We'll find Buddy. We just gotta keep hunting. Come on, let's get the fuck out of here, and go home so I can spank dat ass."

T.J. Edwards

Chapter 6

"You finna make me do dis fa real, Kaleb?" Bree asked, walking backward with her hands covering her ass.

I sat on the couch, patient. I was gone off of a gram of heroin, and two Perks. She was dressed in a pair of pink lace panties, with the matching bra. Her body looked good. "Shorty, bring yo ass over here, and get what you got coming to you."

Bree sighed. "But you heavy handed as hell. Dat shit be burning too bad."

"Shawty, if I gotta get up, I'ma really tear into yo ass. It's best you come on over here and lay across my lap on yo own." I took a swallow from my apple juice. The sweetness of it all, coupled with the heroin flowing through my system to create a perfect blend of euphoria.

Bree slowly came to me. The closer she got, the better I could smell her perfume. She knelt slightly and laid across my lap. "Let's get dis shit over with. It's fucked up that I can't express my feelings for losing my only child. Dat ain't right Kaleb."

"Fuck what you talking 'bout. I already told you that we make other ma'fuckas shed tears. Yo heart is supposed to be blacker than Viola Davis." I yanked her panties into her crease and exposed them hefty cheeks. Bree was every bit of forty inches. Strapped. I rubbed that ass. "Take dis shit like a queen."

"Fuck you, nigga. Do what you gotta do. But just know that after you do dis shit, I ain't fuckin you for at least a week."

"Yeah, we'll see about dat." *Smack*! *Smack*! *Smack*! *Smack*! My hand went right to work tearing her ass up. With each slap, her ass cheeks vibrated and jiggled. She began to squirm all around in my lap. "Ouch! Ouch! Stop! Please!"

More smacking. She kicked her legs wildly until I trapped them between my own legs. Once I locked my ankles, she couldn't move. *Smack! Smack! Smack! Smack!*

"Uhhhh! Please daddy!"

I wore that ass out. It got to the point that she was no longer fighting me. She whimpered underneath me and took the smacks. Her thighs slightly opened. I could smell her scent loud in the air. The crotch band of her panties were soaked. I kept right on smacking. Every now and then I would pat that fat pussy just to see what she would do.

She shivered and opened her thighs further. "Stop, daddy. Stop! Unn. Unn. Unn. Please."

I rubbed the material of her panties into her crease and squeezed that ass before continuing to spank her thick ass. She threw her head back and hollered toward the ceiling.

My fingers found their way into her slit. Two fingers slammed in and out of her at full speed. Then just as she began to enjoy it, I pulled them out and spanked her some more. "What daddy tell you, Bree? Huh? Tell me that I told you?"

She shivered and bit into the couch. I could hear her groaning. Her knees were spaced wide. Juices ran down her thighs, all the way to her knees. "No crying, daddy. You said... No crying, dadddeeee!"

I pinched her erect clit, quickly took my hand away and kept spanking her. "That's right."

She screamed and started to cum hard. She shook against me and placed her knee on the table that was in front of the couch. Now her pussy was bussed wide open. The material of the panties had gotten caught in between her sex lips. Both labia were split in half. The panties were so wet that they were see through. I kept spanking her, until she fell off of my lap. She landed on the floor on her back, with her hand between her thighs, fingering herself at full speed.

I stood up and looked down at her. "Look at you, bitch. Daddy got dat pussy wet, don't I?"

She kept right on fingering. She ran her thumb in circles around her clit. "Fuck you, Kaleb. Fuck you! You ain't my daddy." She rolled on to her stomach, and stood up on shaky legs.

"What the fuck you say?" I snapped, walking toward her. I could see her pussy lips slightly opened. It looked like it was breathing. Her neck perspired.

"You heard what I said. I ain't gotta repeat myself." She made her way down the hallway.

I stood there for a minute lost in my own thoughts. Then I came to. I closed the distance between us, and grabbed a handful of her curly hair. "Bitch, you think shit sweet?"

She hollered, and elbowed me in the ribs. That broke my hold on her hair. "Get the fuck off of me. I hate you right now." She walked off again.

I rushed her and tackled her ass to the floor. She landed on her back. I got between them thighs and yanked her panties off of her while she fought me. She hit me in the jaw twice and once on the forehead. That shit hurt like a ma'fucka, but not enough to stop me from sliding home. As soon as I was in that pussy, I got to fucking her like my life depended on it. My dick beat at her walls like I was trying to knock them down. She was wetter than I had ever felt her before.

"Uhhhh! Get off of... Uhhhh. Shit! I hate you!" Her thighs opened as wide as she could get them.

I sucked hard on her neck. Bit her and kept fucking. "Dis my pussy. Mine! I'm daddy! Me! Only me! Fuck you whenever I feel like it," I growled, trying to split her lil thick ass in two.

"No. No. Shiiit!. Stop. Unn. Unn. Daddy!. Uhhhh! Shit. I'm cumming!" She dug her nails into my shoulder blades and came, shivering with her mouth wide open.

I licked all around her juicy lips. Sucked the bottom one into my mouth and kept pounding away at her. In my head, I was taking that pussy. The more I imagined that, the longer I felt like my piece got. Bree fought me the whole way. She kept right on pushing and clawing at me. The more she fought, the better the pussy felt, until I was cumming deep within her channel. Her nails raked blood out of my back. But it felt so good.

***

We lay exhausted in bed ten minutes later. She straddled my waist and planted kisses along my neck, before laying down with her head on my chest. "Kaleb, I don't feel no better after killing Toni. I thought it would make me feel slightly better, but all it did was make me yearn to get my hands on Buddy. I swear I never wanted to hurt anybody as much as I wanna hurt him."

"I know, baby. I feel the same way. My every other thought is Destiny."

"Which one? Your sister or your daughter that he could potentially have?"

"Both. Dat nigga gotta pay for both of them."

"What if he don't even have your daughter? When are we going to go at Damien, and his dread heads?"

I didn't know. "Baby, my cousin Ajani and his crew doing a lil digging. Once they find out which one has Destiny, that'll be my cue to know which one to go at the hardest."

"So, you're saying if it turns out that Damien has Destiny, Derez and your mother, you're just going to put Buddy on the back burner until a later date?"

"Nawl, just until I annihilate Damien. Depending on how well connected dis nigga is, it shouldn't take up much time."

Bree sat up and slid off of me. She paced back and forth in the room naked. The moonlight that was shining through the bedroom window illuminated her sexy form. "Dat shit sound selfish to me."

I sat up. I felt like I was getting a migraine. I needed another dose of that China White. It was calling me. I got out of the bed and grabbed my dope out of the top dresser drawer. "Shorty, you bugging."

"I ain't bugging. But I honestly think that would be selfish of you let Buddy off of the hook while you went at those Jamaicans. You can't keep forgetting that he took my daughter away from me. She was all that I had. Every day that he gets to breathe, and she doesn't is like a slap in the face to me. I want him gone, Kaleb. I need to be the one to do it. I deserve to be. We gotta find him and crush his ass before we do anything else. Please daddy. I'm begging you." I could hear her voice cracking. She sniffled, hiding her face from me.

"I know you bet not be doing what the fuck I think you is. Are you?"

She shook her head. "No daddy, I'm not. But I am close too. I feel like you ain't paying my feelings no mind. You act like you can't even acknowledge them. I mean, it's one thing to be tough, but to act like losing a child isn't earth shattering is another thing." She slumped her shoulders. "I feel weak."

I slid over to her after putting my paraphernalia back in the top drawer. Wrapped her in my arms. "Baby, your feelings matter to me. I know you're hurting. I know you wanna get this bitch ass nigga back, and we. But until we do we can't allow for him to conquer our every thought. If you know me by now you should already know I don't believe in loose ends. Dat nigga gon get his. I promise you that."

Bree hugged me tighter. "He has to, Kaleb. He has to get what he deserves. He took my baby away. She was so special. She was my little girl. She loved you just as much as I do. Buddy knew that. He knew that and that's why he killed her." She grew weak in the knees and fell against me.

Now I was emotional. I pulled her back up and hugged her small body. "I got you, Bree. I got us. I won't let this nigga get away with his sins. We'll be his plague, ma. We gon give his ass everything that he got coming. That's my word."

Bree nodded. "I love you, Kaleb. I don't trust nobody in this world like I trust you. And I know you got me. I know you will never let me down. But you gotta know that I will never let you down either. Until we crush Buddy, I will never be happy. I will never be able to live with myself. He makes me hate living. Every morning I wake up and he's still alive, but Breeyonna's not I literally want to die." She started to shake.

I picked her up. She wrapped her thighs around me. I began to walk around the house with her. I slightly patted her butt. "I got you, boo. I love you too. We in dis shit together. We finna make dese niggas feel our pain. You just gotta trust my process. Do you understand me?"

"Yes daddy." She snuggled into my neck. "Can you hold me up like dis until I fall asleep? Please? I swear I feel like a little girl again."

"I got you, boo. Gone 'head and rest that weary head. Daddy got you, and I'll always have you. I promise." I walked around the house with her lost in deep thought for the next twenty minutes. By the time it was time for me to lay her in the bed, not only was she out like a light, but she kept on whispering Breeyonna's name. Tears seeped out of her closed eyes. Seeing that broke my heart. I knew I had to slay Buddy for her, and my family. He had hurt one too many queens in my life. That included Rayven. Though I didn't mention her situation to Bree because I knew they hated each other. I felt supreme anger toward Buddy for taking Rayven away from me. He would have to pay in the deadliest way possible. There was no other way around it.

***

The next morning, Ajani was beating on the front door like the police. When I opened it, he dropped his head and shook it. "Kaleb, they just pulled two bodies from the Delaware River. I think it's our people. You gotta get out there to New Jersey right now."

T.J. Edwards

Chapter 7

"What we gon do about dis shit, Kaleb? Huh? Look at my ma'fuckin' auntie, man," Ajani snapped, pointing at the table.

I stood looking over Derez's body. His face looked like whoever had killed him took pleasure in the murder. There were more than thirty holes in his face. I figured they were stab wounds. Much like Destiny, his eyes were gouged out. His ears were also missing. His throat had been slit, from what I could tell, by a sharp knife of some sort. His body was bloated.

I was sick. I didn't know what to say, or what to think. There were so many thoughts going through my brain at the time. I felt like I was about to lose myself.

Ajani continued to pace back and forth in the cramped basement. The smell of Derez was serious. His body was starting to decompose. No doubt the river had sped up the process of that. "Yo, I don't what niggas think it is wit us Kaleb, but we gotta go at these nigga's chin. We gotta make dem Jersey dread heads feel the pain that we feeling right now. Ain't no other fuckin way around it."

I placed my hand to Derez's chest. It had swollen up as if it were getting ready to burst. Bugs and maggots were crawling all over him already. I felt lower than dirt. "Yo, cuz, I thought you said they pulled two bodies out of the River? Where the other one at?

Ajani stopped pacing. "The other one was a nigga, but he wasn't no kin to us, so my men left his ass floating."

"What made y'all go to the river and search anyway?" I asked, looking Derez over. I was worried about my mother. I had already lost both of my siblings. That shit was mentally tearing me apart, but I knew I had to be strong in front of Ajani and Bree. She stood against the wall looking like she was sicker than I was. Shit was getting serious faster and faster each day it seemed.

"One of my homeboys that rotated out of Camden County got a tip. We followed it and sho enough, we found Derez ass floating with his ankle attached to a chain right in the eastern quadrant of the Delaware River. That's where Damien and his boys do all of their importing. That bitch nigga gotta feel dis pain, Cuz. On everythang."

I nodded in agreement. "If he stanked my lil brother like this, who's to say he won't do the same thing to my mother?" That thought made my heart hurt. She had already been through way too much in life. I didn't know what I would do if I lost my mother, especially in the fashion that I had lost my siblings.

"Dat's what I'm saying, cuz. We gotta mount up. Dat nigga Damien done took over 'The Alley' in Camden County. The Alley is infested with all kinds of drugs, Jamaicans, and straight killas. We gotta be ready for war, if we finna go fucking wit them niggas. I got the drop on a few of Damien's main niggas. If we hit them off first, they'll lead us right up to where Damien is hiding out at."

"Why wouldn't we go directly at him? Fuck going through his homies. Time is running out. The sooner we get to that nigga. the better the odds of my mother still being alive when we find him."

"Dat shit don't work like that, Kaleb. Damien is a made nigga. With the shit that he handling over in New Jersey he's able to take care of a whole village of ma'fuckas back in Kingston. They worship his ass like he's a young god. I don't know what you and Buddy did to cross him, but that nigga must have his mind made up to torture you before he send those killas at your throat. I don't think he give a fuck about yo money. If that was the case, he would've had you deliver a Hefty bag already. I think it's personal. He on some mental shit."

Bree stepped from the wall and placed her hand on my shoulder. "So, what do you advise that we do Ajani?"

"We gotta break down the structure to his organization. Take out some of his chosen heads, and slowly make our way up to him. Shit finna get real bloody, and there is a potential that before it's all said and done, we could lose our lives in the process. Before we do any thang, ma'fuckas gotta really ask themselves if they are ready to die for this shit that we are about to get into? Me personally, I'm riding for my family until the death of me. My auntie has always been my heart. She was my mother's favorite sister. So, death ain't shit to me. I'm an Edwards. What about you, Kaleb?"

I continued to look down at my brother's body. A maggot crawled out of his eye socket, and scooted across his cheek, before dropping to the table. "Nigga, I'm ready for whatever. My mother is my life. Whatever we gotta do to get her back, I'm ready."

"Me too," Bree said, stepping forward. "I know that her and I didn't have the strongest relationship, but she means the world to Kaleb, so she means the world to me. I'm ready for death."

Ajani nodded. He smiled and looked over to me. "I like dis bitch, Kaleb. Shawty seem like she 'bout dat life. Hoez like dis is hard to find."

Bree stepped into his face. "My name Bree. Dat's all. Not bitch. Not ho. Nigga, just Bree. You understand that?"

Ajani scrunched his face. "Let me tell you somethin shawty. I'm from the Windy. We call bitches in Chicago bitches, or hoez. Dat's the same shit I'm gon call you. If you don't like it den dat's on you. Get the fuck out of my face before I slap yo ass to the ground."

Bree remained planted. "Nigga, my name is Bree. Dis is New York. Dis ain't no fuckin' Chicago. But even if we were in Chicago, I wouldn't give a fuck what you call dem females out there. You would be calling me by my name. So once again, my name is Bree, nice to meet you." She held out her hand.

Ajani mugged her. He looked past her shoulder, and over to me. "Say Kaleb, fuckin wrong with her?"

I stepped beside Bree. "Shawty is a reflection of me. She ain't 'bout to settle for shit less than yo respect."

Ajani jerked his head back. "Nigga, do you know what I do to hoez?" he asked.

I shook my head. "Nall, and I don't give a fuck either. Shorty rolling wit us. All she asking is that you call her by her name. What's so hard about that?"

Bree nudged me to the side and took a step forward. "Kaleb, I don't need you standing up for me. I got this. I know that nigga a killa and all dat, but so am I. I ain't got no problem with calling him by his name, and he gon do the same for me."

Ajani upped a gun so fast and placed it under Bree's chin. He grabbed a handful of her hair making her yelp. "Bitch, I'm calling you what I call you. If you got a problem wit that, I don't give no fuck. Now pipe yo li'l ass down before I send you to the morgue. You feel what I'm saying?"

Bree remained silent for a moment. She took a deep breath, and slowly blew it out. "Bitch ass nigga, if you gon blow my shit back, then do it. I ain't got shit to lose. All I had was my daughter, and she gone now. So, if you wanna put a fuckin bullet in my head because I'm demanding my respect, then do it. Do it or let me go because you're getting me real mad." She slid the .380 out of her waistband and pressed it to Ajani's crotch. I heard the hammer cock back. "What you gon do?"

Ajani tensed up. He slowly trailed his eyes down and swallowed his spit. His hold released on her hair. He pushed her away from him. "Shawty, just stay yo ass away from me. Somethin ain't right about you." He tucked his gun back into his waistband. He stood beside me and leaned into my ear. "Dat bitch don't know who she fuckin wit, Kaleb. I'll advise you let her know how we get down on my side of the family, or else I'ma perform an autopsy on her ass. Ya feel me?" He looked me up and down. "Now we got work to do. I'm finna follow a few leads out there in Jersey. When I find out the best way to penetrate this nigga's circle, I'll be in touch." He looked down to Derez again and shook his head in disgust. "Dat's way too many losses for an Edwards, Kaleb, and you know it."

"Just find out how we should get at this nigga and reach out to me. I got some shit to handle on this end in regards to my daughter, and Rayven." I scanned Derez again. Now there were a bunch of maggots dropping out of the holes in his eyes. His chest and stomach were so swollen that I knew in any minute, he was set to burst from the Riga mortis.

"Yeah, aiight, cuz. What you wanna do wit his body?" Ajani asked, snapping his fingers. His Ski Mask Cartel killas surrounded the table Derez was laying on.

I stepped forward, moved a bunch of bugs off of Derez's body. Then I kissed my brother on the forehead. "I love you, lil homie. I'll see you real soon." I was sure of that. "Just get rid of him. Don't ever tell me what you did."

Ajani nodded. "Will do."

***

That night, me and Bree rolled around New York in silence for all of two hours, before she broke it. She took a long swallow from her pink Molly-spiked bottled water. Placed the bottle back into the console and sat back. "Kaleb, what would you have done if your cousin would have killed me tonight?"

I was just coming off of the expressway. I had images of the last time I had seen my mother, going through my head. "What do you mean?" I knew what she meant, but I just needed time to think of an answer.

"I mean, if he would've killed me in that basement out there in New Jersey, what would you have done to him? I just wanna know. And be honest too." She turned her body so that she was able to see all of me.

I rolled through the lights and kept rolling. "That shit wouldn't have ever got that far. Ajani can tell how much I care about you. He knows I'm going through a lot. The last thing he would do is cause me any more pain than I'm already experiencing." I made a right turn on to Seventh Ave. "Open that bottle, and hand it to me." My mood was starting to slip. I needed to get some of that Molly in my system. I was already fucked up off of two grams of China, but that tooting shit wasn't getting me as high as it once was. I was still getting sick. Thoughts of shooting my dope was fuckin with me every second of every day. I was feening to do it.

Bree handed me the bottle after removing the top. "Dat's not what I asked you. I asked you what you would've done if he would've killed me in that basement?"

"Yo, if I even thought Kid would do some shit like that to you I would've never let shit progress that far. You fucked up by stepping into his face. That nigga got every bit of thirty or more bodies under his belt. His father, Greed, trained him and his brother Rayjon at a young age to be killas. The fact that you still got air in your lungs is solely because of the respect he has for me."

Bree sat back in her seat as we rolled through a seedy part of Harlem. It looked like a place where the lowest of the low lives went to die. There were boarded up stores, and skinny, sickly prostitutes on every corner. Dirty mattresses were on the side of the road. It even smelled like death. "Yo pull over Kaleb."

"What?" I asked, shocked.

"You heard me, nigga. Pull dis ma'fucka over. I need to be away from yo ass for a minute. I'll find a bus back home. Word up."

"Shawty stop playin wit me. Fuck I look like dropping yo ass off in Harlem? Especially over here. You wouldn't make it two blocks."

Bree popped her seat belt off. She clicked the lock on the door. "Nigga if you don't pull dis bitch over den I'm bout to jump out while you still rolling. But either way, you finna let me up out dis bitch." She opened the door slightly. "Pull it over!"

I slowed the truck down and pulled over on a hundred and forty second and St. Nicholas. "Shorty, what the fuck is you tripping on?"

She grabbed her handbag and climbed out of the truck without uttering a word to me. Four whores that were standing on the corner looked over at us. They began whispering to themselves. "Kaleb, the fact that you don't know says way too much to me. Nigga, I'm through fucking wit you. I hope you go and live your best life. Fuck off." She slammed the door and took off walking down the dark block.

I sat there feeling stupid, and angry as a muthafucka. I didn't feel like dealing with no female's emotions. Bree was getting on my ma'fuckin' nerves. "Fuck, I'ma leave her ass den," I said out loud, and took off rolling. I noticed that one of the hookers were making their way up to my truck before I stepped on the gas. I didn't get more than a half a block away from Bree before I got to imagining something bad happening to her. The image was too much for me. I slammed on the brakes, and threw it in reverse, storming backward down the dark street. When I pulled up on her she was talking on her cell phone. "Shorty, get yo ass back in the truck. I'm sorry now. Come on." A bunch of dudes appeared out of one of the buildings. They were every bit of ten deep. They all seemed to have hoodies over their heads. My antennas went up.

"Drive off, Kaleb. You don't give a fuck about me. That shit is oh so clear. All I got is me. So why keep faking the funk?" She took her cell phone away from her ear am kept walking. I was rolling beside her.

The group of dudes stepped into the street and began following Bree. One of them had dropped his hoodie. He had long dreads and a blue bandanna over his face from the nose down. "Say bitch! What's good?"

Bree stopped, and turned around to look at him. "Excuse you?"

He put some pep in his step. "Come here, bitch, I wanna show you something." His crew followed close behind him.

Bree stopped in her tracks and blew my mind when she began walking in his direction.

Chapter 8

"What you want, huh? Do you know me or something?"

I started to panic. The closer she got to them the more worried I became. I threw my truck in park. Unlatched the seat belt and rushed to the back seat. I grabbed the MAC .90 from under the seat and cocked it.

Boom! Boom! Boom! Boom!

"What?" I rushed to the driver's seat, and opened the door, jumping out of it. What I saw blew my mind. Bree stepped over the first dude that had been calling out to her. He lay in the street holding his neck kicking his legs like he was fighting for dear life. About three feet from him was another man. He lay on his stomach motionless. A puddle of blood already formed under him. She chased the other men blowing at them back to back. *Boom! Boom! Boom!* "I'm tired of this shit. I'm tired of you men thinking you can take advantage of me. Arrgh!" She seemed to be running as fast as she could bussing. All of a sudden her gun was empty. She stopped. She stood in the middle of the street with her gun smoking. The dudes disappeared in every direction.

I don't know if she saw it or not. But suddenly one of the apartment building doors to the left of her opened. Three dudes ran out of it shooting at her. Blocka! Blocka! Blocka! Blocka! They fired with their handguns. Bree ran a few paces and fell to the ground.

"Noooo!" I hollered. I just knew she was hit. She fell so awkwardly. The she wasn't moving. I ran down the street airing. Bocka-bocka-bocka! Bocka-bocka-bocka! Bocka-bocka-bocka! The Tech spit rapidly in my hands. The fire lit up the dark street. The shooters took off running. Occasions they soups stop, kneel behind a car, and fire a few shots at me, before they ran further away. I kept airing trying my best to count the amount of bullets that I let loose as I fired but I lost count almost immediately. When I got to Bree she hopped up. "What the fuck took you so long, Kaleb. Dem niggas could of killed me. Aw shit!" She pointed toward a building. Like twenty Harlem niggas ran out of it with big guns in their hands. They looked both ways. Squinted to see us and rushed into the middle of the street. Then they were shooting rapidly. They sounded like they were blowing fully automatics. We had to get out of there.

Bree took off running first. She made it to the passenger's door and tried the knob. It was locked. "Baby, hurry up."

I knelt down and let off ten shots. I had to let them fools know that we still had led in our pistols poles too so they wouldn't think it was sweet. I got up, and ran to the driver's side, just as Bree climbed in, and across the console. As soon as I got behind the wheel, the back window shattered. Bree dropped to the floor and screamed. "Pull off Daddy! Now! What is you waiting on?"

I stepped on the gas. The truck took four more bullets before I swerved and hit a parked car. The crunching of metal was loud. The car's alarm sounded. I backed out into the middle of the street and took three more bullets to the body of my Range Rover. The driver's window exploded. I ducked down and switched gears. Stepped on the gas and shot off of the block with my heart beating a million miles an hour.

***

When I came out of the shower naked that night, Bree knelt in the living room with a thirty-eight Special in front of her. She had candles lit all around the living room, with incense burning. It took a second for my eyes to be able to focus in on what she was doing. She took a bullet, and placed it inside of the chamber, spinning it. She put the barrel to her temple, and pulled the trigger once, then twice.

I rushed to her and yanked the gun away from her. "Man, what the fuck is wrong with you?"

She stared up at me. "I'm stopping myself from crying." She covered her face with her hands. When she took them away her eyes were still closed. "I can't take this shit, Kaleb. I'm dying on the inside. I miss Breeyonna. I miss her so bad that I don't know what to do. I don't think I wanna be here anymore." She pulled her tank top up and dabbed at her eyes before any tears fell.

I knelt on the rug in front of her. "So, you just wanna leave me then?"

She sniffled. "I'm not strong enough to be here. I need something, and I just don't know what. My every other thought is about Breeyonna. I'm not even sure if killing Buddy will make me any better at this point." She held out her had for the gun. "Please. Give it to me." A tear dripped down the left side of her face.

I couldn't do nothing but stare at her. "You ain't about to leave me in dis world, Bree. Me and you are in this shit together. Do you hear me? Just like you sitting yo monkey ass over there hurting. I am too. I've taken just as many losses as you have. Just think about it."

She ran her fingers through her hair. "I know you have, and I'm not saying that you haven't. What I'm trying to tell you without actually losing it here is that I am not strong enough to continue to feel the way that I am feeling. I feel like I am dying from the inside out. I don't know where to turn, or how much more I can take. So, give me the fucking gun. We gon let fate decide dis shit."

I squeezed the handle of the gun in my hand. My adrenalin was pumping like crazy. I took one of the bullets off of the floor, and placed it inside of the chamber, leaving the one that she had already placed inside of it. "Dis what you wanna do right?" I spun the chamber.

"Waits it was already one inside of it. What are you doing?" She reached for it again.

I smacked her hand away hard. Placed the barrel to my temple and cocked the hammer. "Fuck this life then."

"Kaleb no!"

Click!

She closed her eyes and jumped back preparing for the explosion. When she saw that it had landed on an empty chamber she seemed to take a sigh of relief. "Kaleb!" She reached for the gun again.

I placed it on the carpet. "Your turn." The candles continued to flicker all around the living room. Our shadows danced of of the wall. The smell of wax, and lit wicks resonated in the air, before it was swallowed up by the incense.

Bree looked down at the gun for a long time. "Is dis really how you want us to go, Kaleb?"

"Pick up the muthafuckin gun and spin the cylinder. Put that bitch to go temple a pull the trigger. You started this shit." I said coldly. I felt like I could see black demons all around the room. I felt empowered. I felt like I was ready to go. Fuck living. "Do it Bree. Do it, or I'ma do it for you."

"You ain't gotta do shit for me." She picked up the gun and spun the cylinder. She placed the barrel to her temple. "If this bullet takes my life, I just want you to know that I love you, and I always have." She closed her eyes, am squeezed the trigger.

Click!

She blew out a sigh of relief. "Shit."

"You tired of being here? Huh? You tired of fighting to find these ma'fuckas that hurt our people every single day.

You wanna punk out, and take the bitch way out? Aiight den Bree. Dis shit ride and die wit me. I'm riding wit yo ass to the dirt."

Click! Click!

Bree covered her face again. "I'm sorry Kaleb. I'm sorry that I can't take this shit. I swear to God I wish I could, but I just can't."

"I don't wanna hear that shit. Pick up that ma'fuckin' gun and pull the trigger after you spin it."

Bree snatched the gun off of the ground. "You're supposed to be a better leader than this. You are the man. I am a reflection of you. You got me doing dis dumb ass shit." She spun the cylinder and placed the gun to her temple. "I hope it go off." She squeezed it.

Click!

"Squeeze it again!" I ordered. "I did it two times in a row. You only did it once. Squeeze it."

"No!" Bree hollered.

"Bitch do it!"

"Fuck you!" She screamed and tossed the gun at me. It hit me in the shoulder and fell to the floor.

Boom!

We both jumped. A big hole appeared in the ceiling. Plaster fell down to the carpet. A white cloud of smoke covered the living room.

Bree knelt down and rocked back and forth. "What are we doing, Kaleb? I'm hurting so bad. I can't take this pain. I need to get away from it. Please help me Daddy. Please. I am begging you." She crawled across the carpet, am wrapped her arms around my neck where she broke down like never before.

***

"Just close your eyes baby and trust me. Daddy promise that after this, nothing will be able to make you feel like you're feeling right now. You hear me?"

She nodded. "Yes daddy."

I took a deep breath and couldn't believe that I was about to do what I was going too, but I couldn't see any other way. I couldn't have Bree trying to kill herself every time I turned my back. I needed her to stick around. I needed her to be strong. I didn't think I could make it day by day without my baby.

I held her arm out straight, and slowly slid the tip of the syringe into her. She winced in pain. I took a deep breath and pushed down on the feeder. Pulled the rope from around her arm, then slowly fed her the China White.

"Uhhhh Dad-dee." Her eyes rolled into the back of her head. She licked her lips.

I pulled the syringe out and set it on the dresser next to the bed. "How do you feel Bree?"

She sucked on her bottom lip. "I can't describe it. I feel like I'm being saved from all of the pain. Like God knew that I wasn't strong enough to endure it and he's trying to protect me. I feel numb. I feel free. I love you so much Daddy. I just..." Her head fell forward. She started to snore. A trace of drool seeped out of the corner of her mouth.

I finished making up the works, then followed the same process that I had for her. After the poison was injected into my system there was like a sudden hit of euphoria. All of my pain, and misery left me immediately. I felt strong. A wave of murderous intent began to drown me. My eyes lowered. I grew angry, and then protective over Bree. I pulled her to me possessively and hugged up to my woman. "Listen to me, Bree, I'll kill a ma'fucka over you. You hear me, baby? If that nigga Ajani would've killed you, I would've tortured that nigga, and shit in his mouth. You my bitch. You belong to this Killa right here. You understand that?"

Bree sat up and frowned her face. "Yeah I know dat." Her eyes lowered. She snored for three seconds, then they popped open again. "Dat's all I wanted to hear you say, Kaleb. I already know I'm yo bitch. Ain't no other nigga supposed to be calling me no bitch. You should've smoked that nigga on sight. Cousin or no muthafuckin cousin." She rubbed her hand over my chest. "I wanna kill something, Kaleb. I need to see blood." She lowered her head again and started to snore softly.

My head rested against the side of hers. I nodded. I couldn't help it. It felt like a weight was on the back of my head. My eyelids felt heavy as cinder blocks. But I felt good. I felt like I could see clearly. I knew what I had to do.

Bree picked her head up. "Let's hit up Harlem tomorrow to see if we can track down dis Zeke nigga. My cousin Alannah from Harlem, she say she was gon' do some digging. She was who I was talking to when you pulled up on me yesterday before them Harlem niggas started on that bullshit." She closed her eyes. "You heard me?"

I could hear myself snoring, but I couldn't stop it. Suddenly, I shook out of the trancelike state and nodded my head. "Yeah I heard you, boo. We on dat tomorrow. For now, let me hold you for a minute. I need to absorb some of your strength. I feel like I need you more and more each day." I pulled her into my embrace. We laid on our sides on the bed.

Bree scooted back into my lap. "I feel the same way, Kaleb. I don't know what I would've done if that gun would've went off and took you away from me. I swear you're all I have in dis world. I can't be apart from you, daddy. I hope you know that."

"I do, boo. Now just chill. Let's enjoy this China." I grabbed the remote control and turned on some Jhenè Aiko, then held Bree while we zoned out with murder and revenge on our minds.

Chapter 9

Alannah was five foot six, light-skinned, with green eyes, and reddish, brown hair that was super curly. I could tell she was mixed even before Bree told me that Alannah's father was Arab. She walked into the kitchen to get us something to drink with her ass jiggling like Jello. Not only was she probably the baddest looking female I had ever seen, but she was just as thick as Bree.

Bree squeezed my hand. "Daddy, I love you." She kissed my cheeks and nuzzled up against me.

I wrapped my arm around her. "I love you too, shorty."

Alannah came back into the living room carrying two bottled waters. She was rocking a white and black Fendi skirt that showed off a lot of her yellow thighs. "Here y'all go. I got a box of doughnuts I'm finna bring in here too. Y'all do eat those, don't you?" she asked laughing, a dimple prominent on each cheek.

Bree nodded. "Hell yeah. Anything you got sweet, we want that like A-SAP."

"Aiight cool." She made her way back into the kitchen.

I couldn't take my eyes from her ass. "Shorty, how old is yo cousin?"

"I think she might be seventeen or eighteen. I don't know. Why?"

"Cause she strapped. I can't stop looking at her lil pretty ass," I admitted.

Bree frowned. "She aiight."

Alannah came back into the room. She sat the box of doughnuts on the table. When she bent over, I could see into her blouse. She had on a pink lace bra that pushed her titties up, and out. "Aiight." She sat on the long couch across from us. Her skirt was so short it showcased majority of her thick,

75

golden thighs. "So, what brings you out here to Harlem, cuz?" She looked over to me? Our eyes locked for a moment, then she looked off. I felt my piece getting hard.

"Remember I was telling you about some nigga named Zeke? He supposed to be a heavy hitter out here in Harlem?" Bree asked.

"Yeah, I remember." Alannah flipped a tuft of hair behind her ear. "What about him?"

"Well, it turns out that Buddy supposed to be fuckin with this nigga now. You remember what he did to Breeyonna, right?"

Alannah nodded and lowered her head. "Yeah, I remember. He's a sick bastard."

"Well, we tryna track his ass down and we need your help. I didn't wanna say all of dis shit on the phone. You already know how dem people be in everybody's business."

Alannah nodded. "Well, you might be in luck."

"What do you mean?" Bree asked, optimistic.

Alannah scooted to the front of the couch. Her skirt rode back on her plush thighs. She flashed a hint of pink panties. The crotch looked stuffed. My dick jumped more than a few times. I wanted some of dat lil bitch bad. "Zeke supposed to be throwing a masquerade party tomorrow for his little sister Janine that just got up here from New Orleans. His little brother Tyson go to my school. He say he wasn't inviting nothing but bad bitches. I'm already invited, and I can bring whoever I want."

"What about the kid?" I asked, trying to get another peek up her skirt. This li'l young bitch was killing. Her green eyes made her look too fine. I needed to see what that pussy felt like. I was already trying to find a way to get Bree on board.

"Aw, you good too. Tyson said we can bring a nigga, but not more than two. So, we straight." She looked into my eyes again and blushed when mine trailed down to her legs. She looked down herself and saw how much skin she was giving up. She grabbed the sides of her skirt and pulled it down.

"Aiight den, that sound like a plan. When yo mama gone be back?" Bree questioned, standing up. She stretched her arms over her head and yawned.

"She supposed to be spending a few days over her man house out in Red Hook. She just left a few hours before you came. Why?" Alannah crossed her thick thighs. I peeped through her gap and saw the pinkness of her panties again.

"Cause until then, me and him finna chill here until tomorrow. Where Zeke supposed to be having this party at anyway?" She yawned again and covered her mouth with her hand.

"He supposed to be renting out the Boys and Girls Club up there on a Hundred and forty-fifth. It's huge. It should be a fun event. If you looking for him, he definitely gon be there. I don't know if Buddy will though. I ain't seen him lately," Alannah said standing. "Y'all can take my room, and I'll sleep in my mother's. It's good." She waved us to follow her. "Come on, I'll lead the way."

Bree allowed her to walk past. I caught her looking down at her ass just like I was. That shit made my piece even harder. "Come on, baby." She wrapped her arm around my lower waist and walked beside me.

When we got upstairs to Alannah's room, Alannah stopped and grabbed some extra sheets and blankets from the hall closet. "Huh, dis just in case y'all want some fresh stuff." She handed them to Bree.

Bree stepped into the room and dropped them on the bed. "Yo, word to Jehovah man, I'm hungry. Kaleb, take her lil ass down the way and snatch me up some White Castle a something. I'm starving. I need a nice nap."

Alannah laughed. "Girl, you been yawning since you got here. You must ain't been getting no sleep, huh?"

Bree shook her head. "Not since Breeyonna passed. Shit been real dark for me. It ain't been nothin but nightmares. But it's all good though. I can see light at the end of the tunnel." She closed her eyes. "Y'all don't let me sleep for more than an hour? Aiight?" She yawned again.

Alannah eased out of the room. "Come on, Kaleb. Let my cousin get a lil sleep."

I kissed Bree on the forehead, and stepped out of the room, closing the door behind me. "Yo, come on. I need to get my baby somethin to put on her stomach."

***

Alannah came back to the car and handed me the bag of food. I sat it on the back seat and grabbed the drinks from her next. Those I put on the center console. "What took yo lil yellow ass so long?" I asked, irritated. She had been inside for damn near twenty minutes.

"It wasn't my fault. There was some fat ass white lady in there arguing with those people who cook the food. She had the lines backed up. I was finna just bounce, but by that time I had been in there too long and had invested too much time. Here go yo change." She tried to hand me a fifty-dollar-bill, and some quarters.

"You straight, shorty. You gon head and keep that." I pulled the Benz away from the curb and got into traffic.

"You sho my cousin ain't gon get on yo ass for giving her baby cousin some money? I can tell she don't play dat shit. Especially since she dropped Buddy for you."

I glanced down at her thighs again as we rolled through the city. It was ten o'clock at night, but the streetlights were bright enough for me to be able to check her out. "Shorty, yo cousin good. We in dis shit together. And she ain't leave Buddy for me. We left Buddy for each other. You understand that?"

She snickered. "Yeah, I guess. But thank you for the ends anyway."

"You good." I kept rolling.

"I saw you peeping me in there too," she said, looking out of her window.

"Oh, did you?"

"Yop. I hope you know I ain't nothing but jailbait. I might look grown, but I'm far from it."

"Is that right?" I looked over at her. She was nodding her head. My eyes glanced down to them thick thighs again. I kept rolling for a minute. Then I pulled over to a hundred and twenty-fifth, down the way from the Harlem River. There was a nice perch where we could overlook the city. I threw the car in park and cut the engine. I left the radio playing. That old school Avant serenaded the whip.

"Why we stopping right here? Bree gon have a fit."

"Let me see that young pussy."

She was stunned. "What?"

"You heard me. What, you didn't think I peeped what you were trying to do when you slid forward on the couch so it could push your skirt backward?"

She shook her head. "That was an accident. I didn't even know what you were looking at until I followed your eyes. I just told you I'm jailbait."

"Well, I'll get a good lawyer. I wanna see how fat that pussy is. Let me see if this shit run in the family? Come on."

"You for real?" She looked both ways.

I slid my hand over and rubbed on them thighs. She felt hot. My hand traveled upward. She slowly opened her legs until my entire wrist was under her skirt. My digits grazed over her panty front. She was packing. I pressed into the fabric. Her lips were meaty. "Mmm. Bree gon kill you."

"Pull dem panties down. Hurry up."

She slid her thumbs under her skirt and pulled them down until they were around her thighs. "There."

I leaned over and smelled her scent right away. There was a hint of sweat mixed with perfume. I turned on the interior lights and looked into her trimmed bush. Her sex lips were already swollen. Her pussy was chunky. "Open dat ma'fucka for me. Let me see dat pink."

She arched her back and spaced her thighs some more. Her fingers stole to her crotch and spread her lips. There was a slight trail of secretions as she peeled them open to reveal a glossy pink flower. "Can you see it?" She moved slightly so she was facing me.

I nodded. "Hell yeah." I unzipped my Chanel jeans. My dick stuck straight up through my boxer hole. "Grab this and stroke it for me, or I'ma tell Bree that you showed me yo pussy, and she gon whoop that ass."

"But you told me to."

"Grab it."

She wrapped her hand around my pipe and squeezed. Her hand was so small that she couldn't close it within her grip. She stroked it without me even telling her to. "Damn, this a grown ass man dick right here." She pumped her fist faster and faster.

I rubbed her pussy. Peeled the lips open a lil further and pinched her clit. She jerked forward and moaned. "Dis so wrong. I ain't supposed to be doing dis."

I slipped two fingers deep into her pussy, and she screamed. I watched them go in and out of her at full speed. The car lit up with the scent of her pussy. Her juices ran down on to my leather seat. My thumb rotated around and around her clit until she screamed and came, yelling that I was so wrong. She shivered and kept pumping me.

I grabbed her hair and led her to my lap. She lowered her face and sucked all over my head loudly. Her tongue went around and around it. It felt good, but every time she tried to suck the whole thing into her mouth, she would gag and pull me all the way out. "I'm not that good at giving head, Kaleb. Ain't nobody teach me how to do it. I learned from watching the movies. But this is a lot of meat right here." She tried again. Her hot breath felt good. I kept fingering that tight pussy while she tried to do her thing.

"Shorty, just concentrate on the head. Don't suck no lower than it. You hear me?" I slow stroked her mouth.

She bobbed up and down in my lap. I turned the interior lights back off and took my fingers out of her pussy. She started to suck me faster and faster. I got to imagining what it would look like if her and Bree's thick ass got down together. I imagined them bumping pussies, and sucking each other's titties, and the sight in my brain became too much. I came all in her mouth, grabbed the back of her head while she slurped, swallowed, and gagged.

When we were done, she sat back in her seat with her skirt pulled up. I played with that pussy all the way until we got back to her crib.

***

When we got back in, Bree was still sleep. I sat all of the food on the kitchen counter and pulled Alannah to me. Her forehead rested against my face. I cuffed that fat ass booty and kissed her neck. "You want me to hit this pussy don't you?" My fingers slid into her crease from the back.

She stood on her tippy toes and moaned. "Yeah. But you ain't gon fit. I ain't grown enough."

I pulled my fingers out of her and bent her ass over the kitchen table. Yanked her skirt up and pulled her panties down. I released my monster and rubbed the head up and down her lil slit. Her pussy lips tried their best to trap my piece's head. Her heat seared me in a delectable way.

"Mmm, Kaleb. You gon get us in trouble. What if Bree wake up?"

I slapped that ass. *Smack.* My dick went inside of her slightly. "How dat feel?"

She moaned again, licked the table. "It feel good. I'm scared."

I pressed a bit on her hole. My head slipped inside of her young pussy. Her furnace felt like it was over heating. "Why you scared?" I gave her four inches.

She groaned and arched her back. She clawed at the table. "Please, push it in me. Please." She tried to push back against me, but I held her hips.

"Nall, bitch. First you finna do something for me."

I pushed forward and gave her another inch.

"Unn. What? What you want me to do?"

I pulled out and looked down at my pipe. It was dripping in her fluids. She was so wet that her juices dropped to the floor from the head of my piece. "Come on, I want you to wake Bree up for me."

Chapter 10

Alannah crawled on to the bed where Bree was sleeping. Bree was laying on her back with her thighs wide open. Alannah pulled the cover back and looked over her shoulder at me. I stood there stroking my piece. "Gon head," I whispered.

"She gone snap," she whispered back.

"Bitch, do like I say." I stomped at her.

She turned back around and crawled across the bed. Her skirt was around her young waist. Her pussy lips smushed into one another. Her petals were slightly open. She got between Bree's thighs and slowly lifted her Prada skirt, exposing her nudity. Bree's pussy was freshly shaven. I'd lined myself up in the mirror while she'd shaven her cat in the shower the night before. Her shit was looking real good. I wanted to taste it myself. Alannah looked back at me again.

I took my hand off of my piece and showed her how it was jumping up and down. "Gon, shorty."

She nodded and lowered her head between Bree's thighs. She kissed her cat and licked up and down her slit. I could hear the sound of her oral love making. The way her ass was in the air had me going through a thing.

I walked over to her and rubbed all over her booty while she went to town on Bree. I'd stop rubbing and poke at her cat with my piece. The head would slip past her lips before I pulled it all the way out again.

Bree started to moan with her eyes closed tight. I didn't know if she was sleep, or awake, and I didn't care. The scene was erotic enough for me. Alannah got to slobbering all over her. Bree raised her hips from the bed and let out a guttural moan. I saw that Alannah's hand was between her own thighs playing with her pussy.

I slapped them out of the way and knelt on the bed behind her. "You gon tell if I fuck dis pussy? Huh?"

She shook her head and kept eating Bree. She felt so hot. She was oozing by this point, with her juices leaking all down her thighs. I eased into her halfway. She lifted her head. I took ahold of them hips and slammed home. I was tired of playing with her.

Her tight womb gripped at my piece, sucking him hungrily. I got to dogging her from behind. Grabbed a handful of her hair and stuffed her face into Bree's pussy. "Eat my bitch. Eat my bitch good," I demanded.

She went crazy, munching away. Bree humped up from the bed and rode her face. She started groaning. I could see the muscles in her thighs flexing. Her nipples poked through her shirt so good, I could make out the full areolas on both breasts.

I fucked Alannah harder and harder. The bed rocked back and forth, squeaking and beating against the wall. Bree screamed she was cumming, at the same time Alannah picked her head up and screamed at the top of her lungs. Her young pussy got to squeezing at me like a closed fist, trying to milk me. I sped up the pace. Her face fell on Bree's stomach, going up and down as I pounded her out.

Bree opened her eyes and locked into mine. She gave me a look that said I was a dirty dog before she closed them back. Her fingers slipped into her box. She started working herself over, her digits getting wetter and wetter.

Alannah came again, then started to run from the dick. I fell on her and kept fucking her lil pussy until I came deep inside of her womb. I pulled out and splashed all over that yellow ass. Opened her ass crack and kept spitting until no more came out of me. Then I collapsed on the side of the bed breathing hard. Alannah didn't get up until two minutes later.

She walked to the door and out into the hallway, before closing the door behind herself.

As soon as she was out of the room, Bree slapped me on the chest. Then she turned me onto my back and got to bossing me like she never had before. She didn't even use her hands. She rested her palms on my stomach and sucked me until I came. She swallowed every drop, climbed up on me, and slid her hot box down engulfing me. She bit into my neck, and fucked me for a half-hour straight, like she was fresh out of a women's prison cumming three times before we fell out, both snoring like bears.

***

"Yo, you look good as hell, daddy, I ain't gon even lie," Bree said, sliding her Phantom of the Opera mask over her face.

I had on a black and white tux I had rented from around the corner. I slid the all-white Mardi Gras mask over my face and dusted off my suit. "Yeah, I was thinking the same thing," I jacked.

She sniffed me. "And you got on that Burberry cologne I bought you. Damn. You going all out. You would never think you're on your on your way to lay a ma'fucka down if it came down to it." She kissed my neck, and grabbed her .380 off of the dresser, sliding it into the holster on the inside of her left thigh.

I gave her my .9 and watched her load it on to her right thigh. I didn't know how she was going to manage but knowing Bree she would figure it out. "Look, we gone ease into the party like the average partygoers. Chill for a minute. Then we gon get right on bidness and hunt this Zeke ma'fucka down.

If he fucking wit Buddy the long way, then he gotta know where Buddy is keeping Destiny and Rayven."

Bree shuddered at the mentioning of Rayven's name. "Damn, daddy. I know you gotta get her ass back too, but can you refrain from saying her name? Me hearing her name just make me wanna rebel from this whole situation," She admitted, fixing her cleavage in the mirror.

I slapped her on her ass. She yelped. "You already know what it is, just play yo role. You know can't nobody hold a candle to my baby." I slid in and kissed her on the neck. "You do know that, right?" My tongue licked up and down the thick vein on the left side of her neck. Then I was smushing my front room into her back.

She shivered. "Yeah, daddy, I know. You betta remember dat shit too when we get her ass back. I ain't playin either."

I kissed her neck and backed up, giving myself a once-over in the mirror. "What's already known need not be explained."

"I'm just saying."

Alannah stepped into the bedroom in a purple Prada gown that clung to her top. She looked good. "Y'all ready to go?" She had a pair of glasses that were used as an eye mask in her hand. They were purple and pink with glitter all over them.

"Yeah, we up out dis bitch. Let's roll out."

***

I waited for Bree to slip through the security check point Zeke had set up at each entrance of the party. The dudes had patted me down real good, and I was worried that since Bree was so fine they would do the same to her, and probably go overboard so they could cop their little feels. But after a brief pat down, she did a little harmless flirting to throw them off track and they released her into the party. She slid her arm around my waist, and we walked into the dark hallway where she slipped my .9 back to me. I placed it inside of my waistband, pulling my suit jacket over it. She kissed my cheek. "Let's handle dis bidness, daddy."

The party was cracking. It was only ten o'clock, but already it was packed. The speakers blared a new track by Lizzo that had damn near everybody singing along it seemed. Me and Bree eased into the crowd. We found a spot. She turned her back to me and began to wind her ass into my lap. Even though we were on bidness, I still couldn't deny the fact that she was doing something to me. I loved her body. Always had. It was something about a strapped ass woman to me that drove me crazy.

Alannah came up behind me and licked the side of my neck. Then she eased through the crowd, giving me a devilish look. I already knew I was gon have to wear her lil young ass out later.

Bree turned all the way around, until she was looking me in the eyes. "You know I love you, right?" she asked, grinding into me and remained in step with the beat of the song coming out of the speakers.

"Shorty, I love yo lil ass too." I kissed her juicy lips.

She slid her tongue past my own lips and began to French me. I gripped that ass. It was impossible for me not to when she was as thick as she was. "Baby, Alannah just gave me the signal. I think she found that Zeke nigga." She broke our embrace and pointed through the dancing crowd of people to Alannah.

I took her hand and we headed through the crowd. I kept getting more and more irritated each time somebody bumped into or brushed up against Bree. I was seconds away from snapping out, until I remembered we were on a mission. When we finally made our way through the dance floor, Alannah was waiting by the refreshment table.

"Look, Zeke is downstairs with one of his guys. I don't know his name. I told him I was going to come upstairs to grab a couple of my friends. He said it would be cool. So, come on." She waved for us to follow her.

I stepped in lead right behind her and took Bree's hand. We navigated through the kitchen area and down a long hallway that led to a stairwell. Once there, we ventured down them, and came to a room used for playing pool. There were eight pool tables set up inside. Along the back wall was Zeke. He was six feet even, dark-skinned, with a muscular build. When we came through the door, he turned around to look at us.

Alannah met him in the middle of the room. She hugged him. "These are the friends I was telling you about."

He nodded in a whut-up fashion to me. Then he went right for a masked Bree. He pulled her into his embrace and gripped her ass. "Damn, shorty, where you been hiding this li'l buddy at?"

Alannah laughed. "She just moved here from Memphis," she lied.

Bree nudged him off of her. "Excuse you. I don't know you to be allowing for you to touch all over me like that."

Zeke smacked his lips. "Bitch, you tripping. I own Harlem. This is all my shit. If you gon be staying in my hood you need to know all of that." He reached out for her again.

I locked the door and watched Bree do the best she could to fight him off of her. He jacked her up against the wall with a frown on his face. "Bitch, you think I ain't finna get what I want out of yo ass?" he snarled.

"Get off of me," she whimpered. "Please. I'm only sixteen."

This seemed to excite Zeke. He yanked her dress up and fought himself between her thighs. "Yeah, I'm finna kill this shit."

Alannah and I locked eyes. She backed up. She looked worried. Her nails went to her mouth. "Zeke, what are you doing?"

"Shut up, Alannah. You already know how I get down. I'm welcoming this bitch to Harlem the right way."

I couldn't believe this nigga was finna try and take my bitch pussy right with me in the same room with them. He must've really thought it was sweet. I cocked the .9 and cleared my throat. "Ahem!"

He ignored me. He tried to kiss Bree on the neck, and she snapped. She head butt him hard. He staggered backwards. His nose was bleeding profusely. He dabbed at it with his hand and looked it over. "Bitch, you broke my nose. You broke my fucking nose." He came toward her with a menacing stare. I was about to rush over and get on his ass, when Bree balled up her fist and got to fucking him up. She hit him with two quick jabs, then swung hard with her left hand, punching him in the nose again. Blood splattered against the wall.

Alannah covered her ears and sunk to the floor. "Y'all stop."

I closed the distance to help Bree. She waved me off. "Nall, I got this. This nigga think it's cool to be all over me like I'm his property a something. Aiight den. Come on."

Zeke wiped the blood from his mouth. He threw up his guards. "Come on, bitch. I'm finna kill you."

Bree held her guards to her chin, she eased into his space. He swung hard. She ducked it and came up with a right hook that dropped him to the floor. She stood over him, holding her right fist in the air. "Fuck you thought dis was?"

I straddled him and smacked him four times as hard as I could with the .9. "Where is Buddy?"

His face was a mess. "What?"

Two more licks with the gun. Now the carpet was drenched with his blood. "Nigga, where is Buddy? I know you know. Tell me where he at or I'm finna splash this white carpet with even more of your plasma." I pressed the barrel to his Adam's apple so hard that I could see his skin breaking.

He coughed up a bloody loogey. "Buddy on a Hundred and Forty-Fifth and Lenox. He got three buildings over here. The first three from the corner."

Bree stood over him. Now she had her .380 out. "Yo son, you bet not be lying. What's the easiest way to get in touch with his ass? Huh? Fuck is he doing on Lenox?" She kicked his ribs.

He groaned in pain. "Trapping. He just got a shipment in from some Jamaicans out of New Jersey. He been feeding the whole hood from the shadows. All I do is work for him. That's all I know." His eyes were beginning to swell up real bad.

"What you think, baby?" Bree asked me.

I screwed the silencer into the barrel of the .9. "Come on, nigga, you coming wit us. We finna pay Buddy a visit."

Chapter 11

"He said he'll be here, man. Dis where we always meet at, and there has never been a problem before," Zeke said, with blood dripping down the side of his neck.

"Nigga, you better hope so for your sake. Because if it seem like shit ain't going the way that it's supposed to, then your ass is out," Bree assured him with her .380 to his neck.

I laughed. I had the .9 under his chin cocked, and ready to blow. From my vantage point in the passenger seat, I could see he was drenched in blood and sweat.

"I just meant this shit to be over. Y'all ain't tell me you were going to do all of this. I'm freaking out," Alannah admitted. She sat in the back seat shaking like a leaf.

"Girl, shut up. All you gotta do is sit yo lil yellow ass back there and be quiet. We got this," Bree snapped. I could tell she was starting to get real short with Alannah. I honestly thought it was because of how she kept catching me lusting over the girl with my eyes, but I couldn't help that shit though, she looked so good to me.

Alannah crossed her arms in front of her chest. "I don't know why you being so mean to me all of a sudden. I ain't did nothing to you or Kaleb."

"Bitch, shut up. With that whiney ass voice! Seriously, is that how I sound when I'm getting ready to cry, Kaleb? Is it? Because if it is, please the next time I sound like that, please buss me in my shit." She mugged Alannah.

I laughed. I was already imagining what Zeke's brains was gon look like splashed all over the windshield. That nigga had that coming. If I could smoke Buddy the same day, that would alleviate half of the battle I was faced with. "Y'all chill that shit out and be cool. We gotta stay focused, Bree. We don't know what Buddy and this nigga Zeke got up his sleeve."

Bree nodded. "You're right, daddy." She sat back and turned to Alannah. "Look, just shut the fuck up until we're done handling our bidness, okay? I don't mean to be all rude and shit, but your voice is irking my soul."

Alannah looked offended. "Fine, I won't say nothing else." She began to pout.

Zeke swallowed his blood again. I was pressing the barrel up under his chin real tough. I didn't give a fuck if it was hurting him. I needed him to know we were serious and if he made any false moves I was knocking his brains out of his head. His phone vibrated.

I yanked it out of his pocket and looked at the face. The name across it read, Buddy. "Yo, dis kid right here son. Ask this nigga where the fuck is he at? Y'all shut the fuck up back there." I placed the phone to Zeke's ear.

A thick rope of blood oozed from the corner of his mouth and landed in his lap. Another one followed it. He tried his best to slurp it up and failed. I hit the speaker button. He cleared his throat. "Hello?"

"Don't hello me, fuck nigga. Why the fuck it take you so long to answer dis phone?" I recognized Buddy's voice right away.

Zeke groaned in pain. I shoved the gun upward and gave him a look that told him to shut the fuck up and get it together. "My phone was on do not disturb, man. Dat's my bad, but I'm ready to fuck wit you on dat other side."

Buddy was quiet on the other end. Then he was snickering. "Aw, is dat right?"

Zeke squeezed his eyelids together. I could tell he was in excruciating pain. "Yeah, how long is it gon take for you to get here?"

Buddy laughed. "Aw, nigga, you already know I'm Mr. Harlem. I'm already there." He broke into a fit of laughter. As soon as he started laughing I saw it. A black van pulled up to the left of us and the door slid to the side.

"Y'all get the fuck down, it's a hit!"

Boom!

My gun jumped. Zeke's brain splattered the windshield at the same time his driver's side window exploded. The round from the enemy sent pieces of face and tissue into my lap. It felt like I'd dropped hot pasta on myself. Then the gunfire erupted rocking the car.

Boom! *Boom*! *Boom*! *Boom*!

All of the windows shattered. The car moved from side to side. I fired across Zeke, then opened the door on his side enough to push his dead ass out of it. He dropped to the ground. I threw the car in reverse and stepped on the pedal with my hand. It lurched backward with Alannah screaming like crazy.

"Bitch, shut the fuck up!" Bree hollered. She leaned out of the window, blowing her .380 at the enemy. I jumped behind the steering wheel and stormed away from the shooters, with her bussing until her gun was empty.

"Hey! Hey! You bitch ass niggas. I know it's you, Kaleb. I saw yo punk ass face. It's on, nigga. You hear me! It's muthafuckin on. I'ma slice your daughter up and send you pieces of her, until I'm ready to slay yo ass. You hear me?" The phone went dead.

I slammed my hands against the steering wheel? "That pussy nigga got my baby. He got Destiny!" Fuck, I was sick, swerving in and out of traffic.

"Kaleb. Baby. You gotta calm down or you are going to either kill us, or get us pulled over by the police," Bree warned looking over her shoulder toward the road.

Alannah was sniffling. "Zeke is dead. He's dead. His brains are all over the car. I can't believe it."

Bree mugged her. "Alannah, I swear to God, if you don't shit the fuck up I'ma kill you next! Shut up!"

I eased off of the pedal and hit a side street. We needed to switch whips. There was no way I could continue to cruise around in a car that was Swiss cheesed. There was blood all over the windshield and overall, it just looked fucked up. "Baby, dis nigga got my daughter. What the fuck do that mean?" I asked. My brain was spinning like crazy. I felt dizzy and like I was losing my mind.

"Baby, it mean we gotta fine his ass as soon as we can. One thing for sure is that he ain't touched her yet. I mean I pray to God he hasn't. He said he was going to hurt her. That means he hasn't done it yet. Try to call his stupid ass back and see what he say."

It was worth a shot. I picked up the phone and clicked on his number. It rang and rang, over and over again. Finally, after ringing for five minutes straight, I gave up. "Dat nigga ain't trying to have no conversation. He out for blood. I wonder how the fuck he knew we were with Zeke? He must've been watching us from a distance."

I pulled onto the dark street and grabbed a screwdriver out of the glove box and handed it back to Bree. Bree had grown up with a bunch of rowdy kids in Brooklyn that were car thief experts. She grabbed the screwdriver and jumped out of the car. She wasn't gone for more than five minutes before she pulled back up in a Nissan Maxima. I jumped back in the driver's seat, and Bree jumped in the front with me. "To the cornfields," she whispered.

"You for real?" I asked, already knowing what she meant.

"We ain't got no other choice. It is what it is."

I shrugged my shoulders. "Aiight." I took off rolling, leaving the old car parked on the side street after wiping it down as best we could.

We were rolling for a short while and I couldn't stop my brain from racing. "I still wanna know how Buddy knew it was us?" I said, frustrated.

"Maybe Zeke sent him some kind of a message we couldn't decipher. You ever think about that?" Bree asked.

"Can y'all please drop me off at my mother's boyfriend's house? I can't take this no more. Please? I'm freaking the hell out."

Bree turned back to her. "Alannah, you're my cousin. I love you, but you done seen way too much for us to just let you go. I'm sorry. That's not how the game goes."

Alannah looked into the rear view mirror and caught my eyes. "So, what are you saying?"

"I mean, I don't know how else to say it, other than you gotta go." By the time this conversation kicked off, I'd been driving for thirty minutes. We were on the outskirts of town around a bunch of farms. It smelled like manure and wet grass.

Alannah's eyes grew big as saucers. "Oh, shit. Please don't kill me. Look I'll do anything you want, Kaleb. I'll be your li'l young bitch. You can have me and Bree. I see the way you look at me. I know you want me. Please just give me a chance."

I swerved to the side of the road right next to a cornfield and threw the car in park.

Bree looked like she was fuming. Her eyebrows were furrowed. "So, bitch, what you saying? You think he want yo lil ass more than he do me?" she snapped.

Alannah looked past her. "Please, Kaleb. Don't do this. I can be good to you. You know I can."

Bam!

Bree busted her nose. "You gon keep talking to him when I'm sitting right here? Huh?" She pushed open the door? "Get out and run."

Alannah had blood oozing through her fingers. "Why are you doing this to me? I'm supposed to be your little cousin."

"Bitch, get out and run." Bree ordered again. She pushed at Alannah. "Go! Now!"

Alannah eased out of the car. "Please don't do this. I am begging you."

I wanted to intervene. I didn't think we had to kill Alannah. I felt like she could've been scared into keeping our secrets, but clearly Bree felt another way. She wanted to take her life. Since it was her little cousin, I kept my thoughts and feelings to myself. I was gone miss her li'l pussy though. That was for sure.

Bree cocked her .380. "You got to the count of three to get the fuck out of this car and run."

"How could you do me like this? I'm your Dickinson blood," Alannah screamed.

"One... two..." Bree counted.

Alannah shot out of the door like a rabbit. She disappeared into the cornfield, just as it began to rain. Bree ran behind her. They both disappeared into the stalks. I slid out of the car to see what I could see. I could hear Alannah screaming the whole way. It was pitch-dark. The moon's rays were covered by the dark clouds.

Boom!

"Come here, bitch!" Bree hollered.

Boom!

"Leave me alone! Don't do this!" Alannah hollered.

I leaned against the car. The rain began to pour harder and harder. It popped off of my waves. I ignored it. I was missing my daughter like crazy. I prayed to God I got to her in time. I thought about Rayven, too. But, being that I was becoming so insane over Bree, it was hard for me to go there emotionally. I did pray she was okay though. She was still in my heart, and

I know I owed her for bringing Destiny into the world. When my remorse for Rayven's wellbeing kicked in worse than ever, shots rang out again.

Boom! Boom!

Alannah screamed. Then there were two more shots and silence. I waited against the hood of the car. Bree stepped out of the stalks like ten minutes later. She walked up to me and hugged me. "Let's get out of here, baby. I'm exhausted."

***

We drove along in silence. I could only imagine what was going through her mind. She had just taken her baby cousin's life. I figured she must've been getting sicker and sicker with each moment that passed.

"You know why I had to smoke that bitch, Kaleb?"

I rolled for a few seconds and nodded my head to the Trey Songz coming out of the radio. "Why is that?"

"Because you really liked that bitch. Every time I saw the way you looked at her lil yellow ass, it made me feel so insecure. Here I am standing beside you, bussing this gun every single day, and I still don't think you've ever looked at me like I saw you looking at her. Shit, even she noticed that."

"You tripping," I quipped.

"What?"

"Ain't no female on dis earth got shit on you. The way I looked at her was full of list. She was just a shot of young pussy. After I bust my nut, that bitch didn't mean shit to me. If she did, I would've stopped you from killing her ass, but I didn't, did I?"

She shook her head. "Nall, but I still need to know that I am enough for you. I don't like you desiring other hoez. I should be your one and only desire. We supposed to be ride and die together."

"We are. But just because we are, don't mean I ain't gon see other bitches that I wanna fuck for the night. That ain't got shit to do with how much I love you. I'm just a street nigga."

Bree nodded. "Yeah aiight. We gon test that theory. For now, don't say shit to me. I need to chill for a minute with my eyes closed. I'm feeling sick and I miss Breeyonna. Wake me up when we get home."

"Will do."

I could've argued with her and took things to another level, but I decided not to. I felt like I should've explained myself better. I didn't want her feeling like she wasn't enough because she was. But at the same time, pussy new pussy was just so hard to turn down. Especially if it was on a bad bitch like Alannah. But I figured that because I cared about Bree so much I needed to get better at putting her thoughts, and feelings first. She was special. "Yo, I apologize, ma."

"What you apologizing for?" She didn't even open her eyes to ask this question.

"No reason, just know that you are enough, and that I love you. You hear me?"

"Yeah, I hear you. I love you too. Now give me my peace and quiet."

I smiled and kept rolling. "Fuck you."

"N'all, fuck you. Good night."

***

When we pulled up to the house, I got an eerie feeling right away. I helped Bree out of the car and up the stairs. When we made it to the porch, my stomach was turning over for some reason. We eased into the house. A strong stench of something ungodly attacked us both right away.

"What the fuck is that smell?" Bree asked, pinching her nose.

"I don't know." We eased further inside. I took my gun off of my hip and looked into the living room. What I saw nearly took my breath away.

"Oh my God!" Bree whispered.

T.J. Edwards

Chapter 12

I stepped up to the table and walked around it. I knew it could only be Buddy's work. My heart felt heavy. There in the center of the living room table was Rayven's severed head. Buddy had made it so that her eyelids were sickly pulled out of her face. They were stapled to her forehead so that her eyes appeared bucked wide open. He'd planted a knife in the top of her scalp. It looked like a handle.

Bree stepped beside me. "I searched the whole house. Everything is clear. I think he got in through the back door because it was wide open." She looked down on Rayven. "Damn, that nigga sick. I mean, I never liked old girl, but this is just wrong." She covered her mouth.

"Why would he let us know that he knows where we laying our head? Why wouldn't he keep that shit to himself, and surprise attack us? Something ain't adding up," I said.

Bree nodded. "Yeah, you're right." She rubbed her finger over the staples in Rayven's eyelids. "Damn, he a dog."

I stood there dumbfounded. "We gotta get out of this house, Bree. Dis ma'fucka ain't safe."

"I know? But where are we going to go? The police gotta be on our heels by now. Now that there is a body lying in this house, it ain't got no other choice but to report back to me, because you put the mortgage in my name. Unless we finna get rid of it."

"We ain't got no other choice than to do that." I snatched Rayven's head from the table and carried it into the kitchen. It felt like I was carrying a small turkey. Blood continued to leak from her severed neck. That told me that her kill was fresh. "Bree come in here and grab a black plastic bag."

She followed my orders and opened it up for me, after doubling it with two Hefty bags. "Huh, daddy."

I dropped Rayven's head inside of it and tied it tight. "Ai-ight, let's clean this ma'fucka up as best we can. Then we up out of here."

We did just that.

***

It was four o'clock in the morning and both me and Bree lay on our backs inside of the seedy motel room just outside of Flatbush. I couldn't sleep no matter how hard I tried. I lay there looking at the ceiling. "Baby, you woke over there?"

"Yeah. I can't sleep. I keep seeing Rayven's head. I can't believe Buddy can be so fuckin sadistic. I was with that nigga all dis time and I never saw that shit in him."

"Yeah, well I always did. I just never thought he would use that sick shit to go at the ma'fuckas he was supposed to love. I can't wait to make him reap what he sow."

"Yeah, me neither."

There was silence in the room with the exception of the rain pouring down outside. The constant pitter pattering of the rain hitting the concrete became therapeutic. "Yo, after we ice these niggas we gotta get up out of New York. You know that right?"

"Of course, I do." She sighed. "Kaleb?"

"Yeah."

"Why are men so triflin'?"

That caught me off guard. I laughed, then felt sick because Rayven's image came across my mind again. I felt like I owed her loss more emotion, but for some reason I couldn't muster the mental emotions. I hated myself for it, but it was the truth. "What do you mean?"

"How is it a man can have a woman that does everything for him that he needs her to do? She can hold him down during the roughest times. She can go all out in that bedroom, and yet in still, when it comes to him only seeing her and ignoring all other hoez, he can't do it? That makes him trifling. Explain that to me."

"Baby, I can't. I mean, I think it's just in a man to want to fuck as many women as he can, even if you think about the Bible. Dem prophets back in the olden times had plenty of wives, and concubines."

"What the fuck is a concubine? Are you saying Cuban women?"

"Nawl boo, concubines. That's like a throwback word for side bitches."

"Oh? You ain't making dis shit up, is you?"

"I'd never lie to you."

"I hope not? But continue."

"Yeah, so I think a man just naturally wants to be with other women physically. That ain't got nothing to do with his emotions. A man could fuck two bitches in a day, and still be craving the love and affection from his main bitch. A side bitch or a regular bitch that a nigga fuck, could never take the place of how he feel about his one."

Bree sat up and climbed out of the bed. "Yo, word to Jehovah man, that's bullshit. And I ain't tryna hear none of that's shit. You belong to me. I better be enough. If I even think you feeling another bitch more than me, I'ma take her ass out the game. Den, I'm coming for you. Fuck a side bitch. You call 'em concubines. I'ma call 'em target practice. Let the morgue sort 'em out." She began to pace on the side of the bed. "You know where I am now, Kaleb."

I was tired. I didn't feel like hearing her mouth. "Nall shorty, where are you?"

"I'm in a murder zone. I just don't care about killing no more. Ever since Buddy killed Breeyonna my heart been black. I don't feel shit. The only time I feel anything is when I look at you." She kept pacing.

I sat up and yawned. "Shorty, bring yo ass to bed."

"I'll kill you if you ever hurt me, Kaleb. I'll kill ya ass if you ever desire any bitch more than you desire me. I pray to God you don't think I'm playing with you either." She stopped mid-pace. "Do you?"

I slid out of the bed and stepped into her face. "What the fuck going on with you?"

"I'm just telling you what's on my heart," she said, looking into my eyes.

"Yeah?"

She nodded. "Yeah."

I grabbed her by the throat and slammed her into the wall. We bumped the motel dresser and knocked the Bible onto the floor. I picked her partway into the air. "Bree, you think cause you slumped a couple ma'fuckas that you running shit? Huh?"

She didn't even fight at my hand that was choking her. She stared at me with a sullen look. Her feet dangled. Her eyes were focused.

"You think you a killa now? You gon threaten to kill me, and I ain't supposed to do nothing about it? Huh? Bitch, are you forgetting who I am?"

Still no movement. She stared at me cold as ice. Her breathing was loud coming through her nose. She gagged and remained still.

I dropped her. "You can't keep saying that crazy shit, Bree. You don't have any idea how it feels when that Reaper really gets on you, and he turns your heart black for real. You don't see shit like you used to see it no more. Life and death is the only thing you'll think about all day long. I don't want that feeling for you, Bree. It's too overpowering."

Bree stood up from the floor with her eyes bucked wide open. "Kill me, Kaleb."

"What you say?" I looked at her totally confused and thrown off.

"I said, kill me. I don't wanna be here no more. I can no longer take the pain of the day by day." She fell to her knees.

I was already pulling out the syringe and fixing it up. I knew what she needed while everything was still so fresh in her brain. She needed to be taken away. She needed the China because I didn't have the words for her. "Baby, you're just going through a lot right now. Things are rough, but you should know that I love you. I will never leave your side. It's me and you until the death." I finished with everything and knelt down beside her. "Give me your arm."

She shook her head at first, then extended it out to me. "Here." She winced as I stuck the tip of the needle into her arm and injected the poison into her. Her eyes fluttered and then rolled into the back of her head like I knew they would.

It hurt me to know the only way Bree could cope was when the poison was inside of her system. But it seemed like it was the path we were headed down. It felt like the world had turned its back on us. Like we were the enemy, and we had to find the best way to survive each day. Even if that survival meant by use of our guns. I watched her slowly climb into the bed. When she got on top of the blanket, she laid on her back.

I hooked me up a batch and shot it up. I had been starting to feel sick as well. I needed the fix as much as I hated to admit that. As soon as the drug rushed through my system, I started to shake. The euphoria rushed through me. I placed the syringe on top of the dresser and climbed into the bed beside her. She was laying on her side now.

"Hold me, Kaleb. Hold me tight. I feel so lost. I don't know what to do." She sniffled. "What would make me kill that girl baby? What?"

I held her as tight as I could. I didn't have the words. I didn't know what to say. All I knew was that I was hurting because she was hurting. I didn't like the feeling. I wanted to heal her. I was hoping the drug would've done it for me, but I saw she needed more than that. "Baby, you did what you had to in order to protect us. That's how you gotta look at it. That's it that's all."

Bree shook her head. "Fuck that, Kaleb. I can't lie to you. I wasn't doin' it because of that. I did it out of jealousy. I couldn't stand the thought of losing you to my lil cousin. I hated the way she took all of your attention from me. Every time I saw your eyes wander over to her, I wanted to kill her. And I did."

"Fuck her, boo. She gone. It's all about me and you right now. Fuck everybody, and everything else. You hear me?"

"I miss Breeyonna, Kaleb. Why is God shitting on us like this? What did I do to deserve losing my baby in the way that I did?" Now she was crying. Her emotions had gotten the better of her.

"Life is a bitch, Bree? Life is cold. Dat's why we are like we are. We gotta fight and kill every muthafuckin day to survive in dis world. We just gotta work with the hand that God deals us. It's fucked up that we lost our babies. You daughter and my sister. But maybe God just wanted to take them away from all of this heartache and pain before the real shit hit the fan."

"He murdered her heinously. His own fuckin daughter. The only way God could've saved her from any headache and pain is if He never allowed for her to be born in the first place." She curled into a ball and pulled my arm over her body.

106

I kissed the back of her neck. "What do you need, baby? Tell daddy? Anything you need, I will do it for you with no hesitation just tell me."

"I don't know. I'm mentally aching. My heart is hurting. I don't know how much longer I can take this pain. It's taking over me." She scooted back into my lap. "Hold me tighter."

I did. "Boo, I love you. You mean the world to me. I ride for you. I kill for you. I live for you, Bree. You're all I need in this world. Do you understand me? We are in this shit together."

She began to shake. "I need some more, Kaleb. I need you to help me not feel any pain for the rest of the night." She got up from my embrace and sat on the edge of the bed, laying her arm straight out along the dresser. "Give me some more of that stuff! Please."

I grabbed the works and hooked them. "I'll do anything for you, Bree. I love the fuck out of you, girl. Damn. Tell me you gon fight for me. Tell me right now."

"I'm trying, daddy. I swear to God I am." She lowered her head and covered her face with her left hand.

I gave her another dose. When I pulled it out, she nodded. "Thank you." She laid on her side. "I don't know what I would do without you, Kaleb. I just don't. If you wasn't here, I probably would have..." She stopped and sat up. Her eyes were big as snowballs. She scooted to the front of the bed and fell to her knees.

"Baby, what's wrong?" I hollered.

She fell face-first holding her chest. The next thing I knew, she was shaking like she was having a seizure. White foam began to come out of her mouth.

My heart dropped. I got to the floor and pulled her against me. "Bree! Baby, speak to me!"

She continued to shake like crazy. Her eyes rolled to the back of her head. More foam came out of her mouth. She started jerking uncontrollably.

I picked her up and ran to the bathroom with her. Placed her inside of the tub and turned on the cold water so it ran on the back of her head. I plugged it up. She continued to shake. I felt like I was about to have a nervous breakdown. If I lost Bree, I didn't know what I would do. I didn't think I could be in this cold ass world without her. I felt so stupid. How the fuck could I give her an extra dosage when the shit we were doing was purer than ninety-six percent. This was all my fault. I knelt beside her and slapped her face. Ripped her gown off of her and threw it over my shoulder. "Baby! Please!" I tapped her face some more. She kept shaking, and then she stopped. "No. No. No." I lowered my head to her chest. There was faint pulse. "God, you gotta be kidding me. Please don't take my baby girl. Take me. Take me instead of her. She all I got!"

I looked back down to Bree. Still, she was still as a board. Tears fell out of my eyes. "What did I do? What did I do? What have I done?" I hollered.

Chapter 13

"Ice. I need as much ice as you can give me. Please," I told the Arab man inside of the gas station's bulletproof window.

"We have more than fifty bags. Are you sure you want all of them?" he asked in a strong accent.

"Yeah, man. Please. Hurry up. My baby could be dying," I said the last part low enough so he couldn't hear me.

A younger white dude stood behind me. "Ain't my bidness. But it seem like to me that one of your people done OD'ed," he whispered, and scratched the back of his neck. He reminded me of a doped-up Justin Bieber.

He had a strong country accent. He smelled of must, and cigarette smoke. He continued to scratch his neck. "So, am I right?"

I looked down at him and nodded. "How did you know that?"

He laughed. "Dis here ain't my first rodeo. I been down dat same road quite a few times. I tell you what."

The Arab man tapped on the window. "Hey, do you still want all of the bags?"

I held up one finger and looked back to the white dude. "What was you finna say?" I asked him.

"I was just gon tell you that if it's only a little overdose, I'm sure I can brang your person back to reality. Long as you do a little something for me."

"I pulled out a knot of hundreds. Before Rayven had went down she'd set me up more than a few accounts. I wasn't worried about no money. That was the last thing on my mind. "Look, kid, you help me bring my lady back, and I'll give you five racks."

The white boy shook his head. "Say partner, keep your money. Why don't you do yourself and me a favor? All I want is for you to hook me up with the same dope that she overdosed off of? You get me some of that, and a thousand dollars. We'll call it even. Deal?"

I nodded. "Bet those. Come on."

The Arab man beat on the window again. He held up five big bags of ice in his hand. "You want dis or not?"

The white boy waved him off. "You won't need it, trust me."

* * *

I made sure that Bree was covered up as best as she could before I allowed for him to come into the bathroom. She was still out of it. I could see her eyeballs fluttering behind her eyelids. I jumped up and opened the bathroom door for him.

He rushed inside and knelt on the side of her. He placed two of his dirty fingers on the side of her neck. "Aw man, her pulse is low. She's on her way out. We might be too late."

Hearing those words made my stomach drop into my stomach. My anxiety went through the roof. I felt like I was going to become hysterical in any second. "Look, man, you bring my baby back and I'll give you half a brick of da same shit. Just please hurry up."

He looked back at me. "Dat your word?"

"Yeah. Dat's my word." I felt like screaming because my nerves were getting the better of me. I couldn't imagine life without Bree. She kept me strong. She was my real right-hand. Ever since she had come into the picture and crossed over to me, my heart had called for her deeper and deeper. I needed her. As much as I hated to admit that truth, I felt like I was nothing without her, especially when it came to being in that cold ass world. Every real man needed his rib. I didn't give a fuck what nobody said Bree was my rib.

"Aiight, cool, a deal is a deal." He reached into his inside coat pocket and pulled out a small nasal spray bottle. He stuck it up her nose and squirted the mist. Once in each nostril. Then he took some of the ice out of the tub and ran it over her forehead.

Bree didn't move at first. Then she twitched. Her eyelids began to flutter a lot. She jerked and began to shake uncontrollably.

I pulled him away from her. "Man, what the fuck did you do to my baby?" I snapped.

"Chill, bro. Trust me. It's a good thing. It means that the reversal drug is working," he assured me.

"Reversal drug. What the fuck did you give her?" I wanted to know.

"Narcan. I carry it with me everywhere I go. It reverses the effect of the heroin. I never know when I am going to need it, so I am never without it."

Bree shook and tried to sit up. She opened her eyes. They rolled into the back of her head. More foam came out of her mouth. She clawed at the air.

"Man, what the fuck do I do?" I was beginning to panic once again.

"Nothing. She's fighting it. It should only take a few more minutes, then you're going to have to get her to the hospital. There is no way around it."

"Kaleb. Daddy. Help me!" She hollered, before placing her head over the rim of the tub and throwing up.

***

I stayed in the hospital with Bree for the next two days. She was really going through it. Every time it seemed as if she was getting over the sickness of the heroin, her body would act crazy. Then she would be back to throwing up and shaking. The doctors placed her on Morphine and had already talked to me about prescribing her Morphine tablets when she got out of the hospital, until she could slowly wean herself off of the harsh narcotic. I already knew we had a tough road ahead. I was thankful the white boy had stepped in when he did. I made sure he got his eighteen ounces of China White, and I forced him to take three thousand dollars. I honestly felt that had it not been for him I would've lost Bree for good. I don't know how I would've taken that.

Bree opened her eyes on the third night we were there in the hospital and called out to me. "Kaleb? Daddy? Where are you?"

I was dozing off on the couch. Since she'd been in the hospital, I'd been so worried that I hadn't been able to sleep a wink. When I heard her calling my name, I jumped up from the couch and rushed to her side. "Baby, I'm here. I'm right here."

She reached out and hugged my waist. "I saw her, daddy. She's okay. She's waiting for me. Destiny was there and she told me to tell you she loves you. That she's okay."

I got a chill that ran down my back. "Bree, you tripping. That's just the meds they got you on, baby."

She shook her head hard. "No daddy, please listen to me. I was there. I hugged Breeyonna. She was real. She's happy where she is. She begged me to stay. I wanted to stay, Kaleb. You gotta send me back there. Please, daddy. We both should go." She hugged me tighter, then looked up at me. "Do you believe me?"

I didn't. But I didn't want to hurt her worse than she was already hurting. I decided to play along. "Yeah, I believe you, baby. I'm happy you were able to see her." I kissed Bree on the forehead and rested my lips against her warm skin for a long time.

"Kaleb?"

"Yeah, boo?"

"We gotta get out of here. I don't think it's safe here. I'm tired of being here." She closed her eyes.

I kissed her forehead some more. "We will, baby. I just gotta make sure you are good. Are you?"

She nodded. "Yeah. I am. I just wanna get out of here. I wanna see Breeyonna again. Even the hugs from Destiny felt good. They are in a way better place than we're in right now. You have to trust me when I tell you this." She tried to sit up. After situating herself for a few seconds, she stopped abruptly. "Thank you, daddy."

I rubbed her curly hair backward. "Thank me for what?"

"Thank you for saving my life. Breeyonna knew you were going to pull me back. She said 'Mama, Kaleb ain't ready to let you go yet. He finna pull you back down there. But please come back to me soon. Promise me that you will, and I did, and then you did. You pulled me back."

Bree was blowing my mind. I didn't know how to comprehend that mystical shit. I believed in God, but I really didn't know for sure how much I actually believed. I didn't think there was an afterlife. I felt when you died it was just over with. But the things that Bree were saying were giving me the heebee-jeebies. "Baby, as long as you know she is okay, you should be able to endure this shit down here with me until God calls us home."

"I know, Kaleb. I should. But a major part of me wants to go right now. What are we doing down here that is so spectacular? We're on the run for our lives. We don't know how we're going to go out. It seems every day we have to take a life. So if you ask me, we're doing more harm than good."

She had a point. I continued to stroke her hair. Her edges were more curly than usual. Probably because she was sweating just a tad. There were small lines around her eyes in places I had never seen before. I figured she was just stressing real bad.

"You didn't answer my question, Kaleb?"

I knew what I had to do. Bree seemed too fixated on this whole death thing. I could only imagine because she was missing Breeyonna so much, and that Breeyonna represented to her the purest form of love. I had to find a way to play on her mental thoughts and emotions. "Baby, let me ask you a question. Can I do that?"

She nodded. "You can. Go ahead."

"Okay, so look." I situated myself so that I was sitting on the side of her bed. I took her right hand and stroked it. "Where do you believe Breeyonna ,and Destiny was when you were just talking to them?"

"Heaven. It was obvious. It looked so beautiful. It was indescribable." She smiled and closed her eyes.

"Why do you think God allowed for Destiny and Breeyonna to go to heaven?"

Bree opened her eyes. She sat up some more and looked me straight in the eyes. "They were innocent babies. They didn't deserve what they got done to them. He allowed for them to go to heaven because they were precious angels, and heaven is where they belong." She frowned. Why would you ask me some shit like that, Kaleb? Ain't it obvious?" she snapped. It caused her blood pressure to shoot up on the monitor.

"Calm down, boo, I'm just making conversation. You're okay," I said, rubbing the side of her face.

She brushed my hand away. "Nall, screw that. You're never just making conversation. Where are you going with this?"

"Well, first of all, I agree with you. Heaven is where those precious angels belonged. God had to send them back to him because they were pure, whereas we are not."

We were both quiet in the room for a brief second. The machines beeped. I could hear one of the doctors being paged on the intercom system.

Bree lowered her eyes and trained them on a spot on the wall behind me. It was like she was trying to avoid looking at me. "So, you think we going to hell, Kaleb?"

"Baby, we been whacking ma'fuckas left and right. Killas don't go to heaven. They go to hell. More than likely that's where we are going. It's common sense."

Bree shook her head. "No, it ain't, Kaleb. If I'm going to hell, then that means I will never be able to see my daughter again. If that's the case, then it ain't right. Breeyonna is all I have, and she is waiting for me to come back to her." Now her blood pressure was through the roof. The machine started to beep like crazy. "Why would you tell me some shit like that, Kaleb?"

"Bree, calm yo ass down. Yo ma'fuckin' blood pressure going through the roof."

"I don't care! Answer my fuckin question. Why would you tell me something like that? What is your angle?"

"Baby, all I'm saying is that you need to fight beside me. I'm here right now. We are all that we have. I don't know if we'll end up in heaven, or hell. But we don't need to be thinking about that shit until way down the line sometime."

"But why would Breeyonna tell me to come back if I couldn't? That makes nonsense whatsoever. You know it doesn't."

"You're right." I didn't feel like arguing with her any longer. It was clear that she had her mind made up. The more I seemed to poke at her the worse off it appeared she was turning physically. "I apologize for what I said."

"You should. Because I don't know how I am going to get to heaven, but I will as long as I can be with Breeyonna. She needs me."

I nodded. "You're right, baby. But suicide ain't the way to go. You should know that for sure."

"But I'm ready to go now. Fuck dis world!" She slammed her fist on to the bed. Now her blood pressure machine read one-fifty over a hundred. I knew that had to be high.

"Calm down, baby. Please," I said softly.

Just then a dark-skinned black nurse came into the room. She rushed to Bree's side, and guided her to lay backward. "Come on, sugar. I need you to calm on down. Your levels are very high right now. Maybe you need a sedative," she said, looking at the monitors.

Bree laid back and closed her eyes. "How much longer am I going to have to be in here?" she questioned.

"Well, we have to keep you for at least another twenty-four hours just to observe you. Then we can release you back to the public after they assuming that your levels return to normal, which right now they aren't. That's not the only reason I came back here either. I don't know how you're going to take this next set of news, but I think it's imperative that you know, considering your lifestyle. Can I speak freely in front of him? Isn't he your spouse?"

I nodded. "Yeah, I am. You can say whatever you gotta say to her in front of me, gon head."

"I'm sorry, but she's going to have to tell me that," the nurse reprimanded me.

"You good. Yeah, he my spouse. We don't keep no se-crets," she said dejectedly.

"Cool. Then I think you should know that you are preg-nant. You're only a little bit along. Maybe five weeks, but pregnant nonetheless."

Bree's eyes popped wide open. "Are you serious?

"Yes honey. So, I think it's time that you change your life-style or it's going to affect your unborn child significantly." She smiled warmly. "I'll give you two a little time to talk." She left out of the room.

She held her head down. "Kaleb, don't say nothing to me right now. I just need to think."

"Baby, I think that's God's way of..."

"Daddy, please! Just go. I need to think this shit over!" she screamed.

I was done with all of that noise. "Aiight, Bree. I'ma give you twenty-four hours. I'll be back then."

She laid back and pulled the sheet over her head. I could hear her whimpering already. I didn't know what to do so I left, just as Ajani hit my phone telling me he needed to see me urgently.

Chapter 14

"We got three addresses where Damien could be laying his head. I say we hit up all three until we find him. Word on the streets of Jersey is that he looking to make a meter with some Dominicans out of Miami. At first, their families were at war. But somehow Damien found a way to squash all that shit, and it's all about the money for them now. We need to get up with this fool before he get too strong. You know what I mean?" Ajani picked up the rolled hundred-dollar-bill and placed it inside of his nostrils. He cleared half of a line of China, then stopped, and finished it with his other nostril.

I was faded. Unbeknownst to him, I'd already shot up a gram of White. My eyes were low. My heartbeat was slow. I felt like I was floating on air. The whole thing with Bree was getting to me. I never thought she would react in such a depressed state at finding out that she was about to have our child. That made me feel some type of way. "Yo son, I'm ready for that hot shit. If your research is correct then we gotta get on bidness like A-SAP. I'm 'bout that. Any word on my people?"

Ajani nodded off. He started to snore loudly. Suddenly he jerked awake and ran his big hands over his face. "Nall, mane, but we looking. Ever since Derez showed up like he did, I been fearing to put too much pressure directly on Damien from fear he would off my auntie. My mother would flip if that happened."

I nodded. "Right." A part of me wondered if my mother was even still alive? She was already sick from cancer. I knew Damien wasn't taking the time to give her the medication she needed on a daily basis. Second to that. If he would kill Derez, who was a young kid, I was thinking why wouldn't he take my mother off of the earth if she deemed to be more of a liability than anything else? It simply made no sense to me. "Say cuz, when you tryna holler these locations?"

"First thang in the morning. We gotta catch Damien's traps off guard." He looked around the dark basement. There was a red light bulb screwed in that served very little purpose in regards to illuminating the room. His Ski Mask Cartel crew stood along the walls with masks over their faces, and fully automatics in their hands at the ready. "Yo, Kaleb, let me holler at you over here for a minute."

I reluctantly stood up and followed him into a more humid part of the basement. The heat increased my high and had me feeling almost suffocated. Sweat slid down my forehead. I popped my shirt to get a bit of a breeze to come into it. "What's up, Ajani?"

Ajani looked over my shoulders at his crews then leaned into me. "Dawg, I heard Rayven had all type of money put into accounts for you and her. I ain't talking about no chump change either."

I frowned. "Yeah she did. But why is that shit relevant?"

He placed a finger to his lips to shush me. "Calm down nigga. I'm just trying to figure something out real fast. Ain't no need for you to freak out."

"Like I said, how is that shit even relevant?" Now my back was sweating.

"Cuz kid, my cartel got a few ventures that we trying to jump into. Moves that could gross us all a whole lot of money. Instead of me kicking doors in and looking for venture capital, why wouldn't I just come to my cousin and you bless me?"

I winced. I was highly offended. "Nigga, don't you understand that a ma'fucka just killed my sister, and my little brother? Then my mother been snatched, along with my newborn child? Nigga, the last thing I'm thinking about is funding some silly ass venture for you a yo niggas. You got the game fucked up, Ajani, come on now."

Ajani held his silence. He clenched his teeth off, and on. "Nigga, so what you saying? You thinking that all of this shit is just free doe? I mean I dome pulled my niggas from Chicago to come all the way out east so they can handle bidness. They losing major money every minute that they away from our Traps back home. You telling me that you can't out a lil bread up as an investment? Fuck type of shit is that? That don't sound right at all." He stepped into my face.

"Boy what?" I pressed my forehead against his. "Nigga, don't let that dope that you tooting make you forget who the fuck I am. Ain't shit cavity like over here. It ain't sweet my Nigga. Believe dat."

Ajani pressed his forehead against mine real hard. He mugged me for a moment, and then busted up laughing. He slapped me on the back. "Nigga, I'm just fuckin wit you. I know there is a right, and a wrong time to do everything. I'm just letting you know though that when we finish your side of things I need for you to invest in me. Deal?"

I eyed him with utter disdain. "Fuck waiting to hit his traps in the morning. We need to hit one of dem bitches right now."

Ajani clench his teeth. His jaw muscles seemed to work overtime. "Yeah, I feel you on dat."

I walked away from him and bumped his shoulder a tad. I didn't like the aura that was coming off of him. Something about him seemed very foul to me. But I couldn't quite put my finger on it.

***

That night, Ajani pulled up in a stretch Lincoln Navigator. He jumped out the back seat of it and walked up to me with a fresh tuxedo on. "Oh boy, don't you look oh so spiffy." He complimented me.

I was dressed in an identical tuxedo. We looked like two high priced limo drivers. "Dawg, why the fuck we dressed up like this? I feel awkward as fuck." I was a street nigga. All that suits and tuxes shit made me feel like a lame.

"Dis how we finna get at a few of his henchmen that's coming from the Lil Pump and Damien Marley concert tonight. I know sit sound crazy, but you just gotta trust me on dis shit. Ain't no fuckin way we was gon be able to catch any one of his traps off guard this early at night. Whereas this way, I got an inside bitch that's twerking shit from the inside. Let me and her work our magic. Huh." He handed me a big game hunting knife that was still in its sheath. It had a compass on the bottom of it.

I took the knife and slid it into my inside coat pocket. "Yo, so how dis shit finna go, Kid?"

"We acting as chauffeurs. The people we picking up are two of Damien's sons. His second and third child. They gon be with a few bitches. They are just coming from the concert. Now, the bitch that's gone be with his second oldest is working with us. She from Camden, by way of the Windy City. Her loyalty is to me and this Ski Mask Cartel. We spare her. If his sons give us the information to find him, then we can spare them as well. If not, then we make examples out of all of their asses. No harm no foul." He ran his hand over his deep waves. "Now, Damien sent for this limo to pick his children up. We intercepted it. We also got one of his crew members from his lower level security team working with us. He's connected enough to pick up Damien's kids, but not enough to know just where Damien is laying his head off guard. Remember, Damien is Jamaican's food, and money supply right now. He's very important. This is why we gotta take shit slow and make strategic moves. Me and you gone chill in the back and cater to his children's commands until we go into action. Just follow my lead."

I didn't like following no nigga. I was a leader in my own right. Lucky for Ajani, I didn't fully understand what he was up to so I thought it was in my best interest to let him take the front, while I stood in the back, and peeped game from close, but afar. "Aiight cuz, do what you gotta do then. I'ma take your lead."

He smiled and dusted his suit off. "Dat's all I'm taking about right there. Come on, let's roll out."

***

I sat with a bottle of Moët in my hand, filling up Damien's sons' glasses, along with those of their dates. His boys were both dark-skinned with long dreads, and brown eyes. They had a bit of weight on them, with strong Jamaican accents.

His oldest son put his glass in my face. "More of dat good shit, mon. Me tink I'm just now starting to feel da buzz." He puffed on a blunt that was as thick as a marker. The ganja was loud, but for some reason it was hurting my head.

I filled his glass. "There you go lil homie."

"Excuse you?" he said, wiping his nose.

"Nothing man. Just there you go."

His brother mugged me. "Say mon, ya ain't no big homie of ours. Ya no ting more den da help. Stay in yo lane," he ordered me.

Ajani laughed. "You li'l young niggas need to have more respect for yourselves, and for my coworker, than that."

The older of the sons flipped his long dreads behind his back, and snickered. "Who the fuck is you supposed to be, his bodyguard or something like that?"

Ajani eyes him with murderous anger. "N'all, dis my cousin. I just don't like how you hollering at him, Dat's all."

"Well, we don't give a fuck what you like." Said the younger of the two. "Yo job is to treat us like kings and shit the fuck up. Y'all ain't sitting back here with us so you can chop it up. No Mon. Ya sit here because we need us too refill our glasses, and to do shit dat we don't feel like doing. Dat's it, dat's all. So shut the fuck up, and keep it coming."

Ajani smiled and the next thing I knew, he shot across the back of the big limo, and grabbed the older of the two by his throat. Both light-skinned girls screamed. He slid a big game hunting blade slowly across it until blood ran into the collar of Damien's second oldest son. "You need some fuckin respect, lil bitch nigga."

He swallowed. "What the fuck?"

I grabbed my knife and followed his lead. I grabbed the youngest son of the two by his dreads and placed the ridges to his throat. "Where the fuck is your father layin' his head?"

He closed his eyes and struggled to breathe. All of a sudden, he started wheezing louder and louder. Then he was coughing. He grabbed his chest and cleared his throat. His breathing became normal again.

Ajani laughed. He slowly slid the blade across the oldest son's neck. A trickle of blood seeped from the wound. The two girls where whimpering and hugging each other. "Where is your father laying his head right now?" Ajani hissed.

The oldest closed his eyes. Tears rolled down the sides of his face. Ma khant' tell you dat. He's my father, and your intent is to hurt him. I can tell dat as clear as day. "

"Aww, how admirable." Ajani sliced the blade across his throat, then all the way up to the back of his head.

Damien's son kicked his legs and acted like he wanted to break free. "Aw, shit man?"

Ajani poked his finger into the neck wound and ripped the skin further open.

The man screamed like a bitch. Blood oozed down his shoulder and drenched his Supreme fit. His eyes were bucked wide open as if he had not experienced such pain before.

Ajani wiped the bloody blade on his cheek. "Where is Damien?" He hissed.

The younger son trembled against me. He passed gas. Then he looked both ways as if he were searching for an escape route.

"Bitch nigga, keep yo ass still," I ordered him. The China White had me all in tune with what Ajani was doing to his brother. The blood excited me. I wanted to see more of it.

"My Pops ain't in the country right now. He in the islands. I swear," said the oldest of the two.

The younger kept trembling. "We ain't got shit to do wit the bidness side of things. Let us go. Please, mon."

Ajani sliced the older across his face with his blade five quick times and stabbed the knife into his thigh. "You think we stupid?" he roared.

The older of the two was hollering so loud that it gave me an instant migraine. The females were trembling like crazy, and the younger son looked like he was on the verge of becoming hysterical.

"Okay! Okay! My father is in Camden. I'll take you to him. Just please get that fuckin knife out of my thigh. I can't take it!" Tears welled up in his eyes.

The younger sim frowned. "Have some fuckin pride. You're acting like a bumbaclot, bitch boy!" he snapped.

"Oh, is that right?" Ajani asked. "Cuz, make him feel some pain for me."

Before he even finished his words, my knife slammed into the youngest's own thigh. I pulled it backward, creating a rip in his muscles and tissues. It opened like a mouth. Blood bubbled up and leaked over on to the seat. I expected his to scream bloody murder, but instead he remained still.

"You can give me pain, but you will never have my pride. I am a warrior." he said, with his eyes closed.

Ajani busted up laughing. "Man, fuck dude. Whack him, cuz. He gon be a problem. Whack his bitch ass right now. Matter fact. Get him." He didn't even give me a chance to make a decision. He shot across the aisle with his knife raised like a mad man. He swung it downward hard. The blade landed in the youngest cheek and shredded it. Now he hollered out in pain. Ajani straddled him and began stabbing him over and over again. "How 'bout dat pride now? Huh? Huh? Huh? Huh? Huh? Muthafucka! Huh?"

I held his crying older brother. He shook against me and threw up all over the limo's floor. "Don't do dat to me. I wanna live. I wanna live. Please!" he screamed.

Ajani finished, and sat back breathing hard with his chest heaving up and down. "Dat's how you shut a ma'fucka up. Hollering all dat pride and shit. Now nigga, if you wanna live, you'll take us to where Damien is. No more games."

He nodded his head. "Okay."

Chapter 15

"I still think we should of went directly to the crib that his son saying he at. I wanna get dis nigga out da way. I'm tired playin games with these Jamaicans," Ajani said, looking up at me.

I finished tying the duct tape on Damien's sons' wrists. I had already secured his ankles. He sat in the basement bound to the chair. His mouth was also duct taped. "N'all, if it's one thing I learned in my experience of trapping out here in New York is that you can't trust them Jamaicans. Them ma'fuckas always got a trick up their sleeve. The only ma'fuckas craftier then them is the Haitians."

Ajani mugged me. "So, what's yo con then, nigga? What is you up to?"

"I say we see how much he really love his sons. If he love them enough, he should be down to give me my mother back. If not, then we off this nigga, and go at his chin. Either way, it go well be able to tell what he's up too."

"Man, fuck all dese head games. I wanna smoke them fools and take over that lil turf they got out there in Camden. Dat's my old man stomping grounds anyway. It'll feel good to put that land back under the Ski Mask Cartel," Ajani said, sitting on the couch and popping two Perks. He grabbed his water bottle off of the round table that was covered with China White residue and pistols. Chugged half of it, before burping.

"Yo, if all goes well, you can do whatever you wanna do with that land. All care about is my mother. Once I get her back, I'm willing to do whatever you wanna do."

"Now that sound like a plan." Ajani hopped up. He walked in front of Damien's son, and slapped his face hard.

The man groaned and hollered into the tape. He tried to break his binds. When he saw there was no possible way of doing that, he remained still.

Ajani ripped the tape off of his mouth. "Say homie, what's yo name?"

He mugged him with his mouth dripping blood. "Fuck you wanna know my name foe?"

"Cuz, I like to know the names of all of the niggas I kill," Ajani snickered.

I didn't have time to be playing games. I wanted to use Damien's son to get my mother back. If I could do that, then at least I would have one very important member of my left. One that I could love and cherish. "Look, lil homie. It's fucked up what happened to your brother, but that shit over with. Yo father killed my brother first, so nigga, it's an eye for an eye. That's how the game goes."

"What?" Ajani looked irritated. "Man, fuck dis nigga. We don't negotiate with terrorists." He punched the man in the jaw and brought his blade back out. He took ahold of his dread locks. Yanked them back so hard, his neck popped. "Say nigga, I ain't gon ask you again. What is yo name?" He poked into his skin with the tip of the blade. A trickle of blood appeared.

"My name Della. Fuck mon. Ya happy now?" he asked in obvious pain.

"You muthafuckin right. Gon head, and ask him yo questions, cuz," Ajani said, nodding to me.

I stepped in front of Della. "Have you seen my mother, Della?"

"What? No." He groaned because Ajani was pulling harsher on his dreads.

"She is sick. Your father, Damien, took her hostage, along with my little brother Derez. He killed Derez and tossed him into the Delaware River. I need to know if he still has my mother or if he killed her as well?"

"Yeah nigga, so answer that question," Ajani ordered. He sliced a short line into Della's forehead.

"I saw her. I saw her and your brother, but I don't know what he done with them. My father keeps me and my siblings away from the business side of things. He wants us to have a normal life, yeah. So, I couldn't tell you what took place with your mother."

Ajani clicked his to his against his teeth. "That's too bad right there, Joe. If you can't tell me what's good with my auntie, then I'm finna automatically assume the worst of the worst. That means it's gone be all bad for you." He looked over to me again. "Kaleb, I'm finna waste this nigga. He ain't doing shit but wasting our time." He raised his knife in the air. Della closed his eyes tight, expecting the blade to penetrate him.

"Wait, cuz." I rushed over and grabbed his wrist.

"Get the fuck off of me," he snapped. "Why are we waiting, and playing around with this nigga? That makes no sense."

"Because I wanna see if Damien will be willing to trade a life for a life." I picked up Della's phone, and scrolled down the log until I saw Damien's numbers. There were three of them. "Which one of these gets into direct contact with your father?"

"A Jamaican is supposed to be willing to lay down his life for pride. For his dignity and for those he loves. I failed my brother. I should've died in his place."

Ajani smacked his lips. "Nigga, you can die right beside him as far as I'm concerned." He yanked ahold of his dreads again and bared his bleeding neck.

"So, what are you saying, Della? Are you saying you aren't going to give me your father's direct number?" I asked, growing impatient. If I couldn't get into contact with Damien, then there was no way I could make a deal with him. If I couldn't make a deal with him, then Della was dead weight. Me and Ajani would be forced to go about tracking him down the old fashioned way.

"Use the one that starts in all threes. It's his direct emergency line. Only his closest family has it," Della assured me.

Ajani sighed. "Man, I hope this shit ain't finna take a million years."

He rolled his eyes.

I scrolled down and clicked on the number. It rung three times before a deep Jamaican voice picked it up. "Della, what is the emergency now, boy?"

Della was quiet. I cleared my throat. "Damien."

"What, who iz dis?" he asked, sounding confused.

"This is Kaleb. I do believe you are holding somebody that belongs to me?" I said, sounding as calm as I could.

"Kaleb? Why the fuck do you have me son's telephone? Dat's how you wanna play da game den?" he asked, with a hint of anger in his voice.

"My mother, Damien? Where the fuck is my mother?" I asked, feeling myself becoming furious that any man would put his hands on my mother. Let alone take her hostage and kill Derez in the process.

"Put my children on the phone you bumbaclot dead man. Do it now! Let me speak to Della!"

"Bitch nigga, let us speak to my auntie. What make yo punk ass kids more important to you than she is to us?" Ajani hollered.

Damien was quiet for what seemed like ten minutes. "Greed, is that you? I thought you were in the pen. You wanna fuck wit me again?" He roared.

"Dis ain't no muthafuckin' Greed. This is his son. You got my aunt, nigga. You done already killed my lil cousin. So, what's yo problem?"

"Greed's son? Who? Fuck that. Let me talk to Della. Why do you have his phone?"

"Where the fuck is my auntie?" Ajani asked him again.

"Della, you be strong, my son. You don't let them break you. If it comes down to it, you die with honor. Long live Kingston."

"Die? Pops, what are you talking about?" Della questioned. His voice seemed to break up.

"Greed, or whoever you are, you have just started a war that you will never be able to win." The line went dead.

Ajani looked over at me. "Dude left his son to fend for himself. Fuck type of shit is that?"

"Call him back. Tell that ma'fucka we wanna do a trade off," I said.

"It's no use. He won't answer. I just accept my death with pride. My father abandoned me, just like he did my older brother, Larky." Della lowered his head. "Give me what I got coming."

Ajani pulled a .45 out of his waistband and aimed it at Della's head. "You ain't said shit but a word."

"Wait, cuz. Damn. Quit being so ma'fuckin' trigger happy," I snapped at him.

He lowered his gun. "Dis nigga useless now. Might as well knock his ma'fuckin' head off."

"Nall. We ain't gon do him the same way his pops did him. That shit ain't right." I gave Ajani the eye. It took him a few seconds, and then he caught on.

"Yeah, you right. That is bogus." He put his gun away.

I knelt beside Della. "Look, li'l homie. It's been enough killing, and bloodshed. We need to cease this shit. Yo pops killed my little brother, and we took your brother's life. We're even if you ask me. I say we move forward. I'll let you go if you tell me where your father is keeping my mother. All I want is my old girl back. Dat's it."

Della lowered his head. "In Kingston, we die with pride. We accept our fate as warriors. To dodge the inevitable is to be bigger than God."

"N'all, li'l homie. It you don't die by our hands tonight then it wasn't meant for it to happen. What is written has already been written. We can't change that. But I am telling you that I don't want to kill you. I want us to cease all his back and forth shit. If you help me get my mother back, I'll let you live and go about your business. You have my word on that."

"But what about my pride? I am a warrior," Della said with valor.

"Man, stop it. Nigga, yo pops been putting that dumb shit in your head your whole life, then when it comes down to it, he threw your ass to the wolves for you to meet your death. That ain't cool, and it ain't love. Think about it," Ajani said, frowning?

Della swallowed his spit. He shook his head. "Who's to say that if I help you, you won't wind up killing me anyway?"

"Dat shit ain't gon happen. If you help me get my mother back, you have my word that you'll be able to walk away with your life. I mean that shit."

"Yeah, lil dawg. After seeing how your father shitted on you, we ain't got no beef with you no more. It's just about us recovering my aunt, and we gon go about our bidness. It's way too many people getting hurt in the cross-fires. You feel me?" Ajani said.

Della kept his head lowered. "If I turn my back on my family, where will I go? How will I survive?" he questioned.

"I'll hit you with a nice chunk of change for you to disappear, and we'll go from there." I rested my hand on his shoulder. "All I ask is that you trust me. I know it's gon be hard for you too, but in this situation we are all we have, and all we have is our word."

Della nodded at Ajani. "And what 'bout dis one? Dis bumbaclot is so ready to kill anybody with no regard. Who's to say that after he gets what he wants dat he won't kill me like he did my brother Raynor?" he asked with hate in his eyes.

"Say boys, I know Bumbaclot is another word for bitch. You betta watch yo tongue, nigga. I don't give a fuck what deal you making wit my cousin," Ajani spat.

"You see? How can I trust a man with such a temper?"

"I'm not asking you to trust him, Della. I'm askin' you to trust me. My mother is everything to me. She is my world. If you help me get her back there is nothing that will happen to you. You have my word on that."

Della continued to mug Ajani. Then he closed his eyes. "Okay. I'll get her back for you. But you better keep your word. In fact, I still have one person in this world that I trust, and one that I know will never betray me under any circumstances. My sister, Mesha. You let me call and talk to her. She will bring your mother to a location and release her. Then you two will do the same for me. We will both be released at the same time. How does that sound to you?"

"How do you know my mother is still alive?" I wanted to know.

"She is. I fed her this morning. She is getting stronger. She is a stubborn woman, but one with great wisdom. I admire her." Della said, swallowing the lump is his throat.

To hear my mother was still alive gave me so much hope, as euphoria to my brain that I felt like breaking down. I needed to see her. I needed to make sure that she was okay. I missed her so, so much. I had lost my siblings, but my mother would be sure to fill those voids as best she could. "Listen to me. Take me to her, and you can go about your business. That's my word. Huh, call Mesha and set it up." I tried to hand him the phone.

Ajani took ahold of my wrist. "Cuz, are you sure about this?"

I yanked my wrist away, along with the telephone. My mother was heavy on my mind. "Yeah, I'm sure. You just be ready in case anything goes wrong. Huh Della, make the call."

Ajani stepped back with an angry scowl on his face. "Nigga you try anything fishy and I'll finish yo ass, then I'll be to see Mesha. Trust me on that."

Della eyed him with hatred. "Leave my baby sister out of this."

I cut his right hand free so he could dial. "Just hurry up before Damien kills my moms."

He nodded and proceeded to dial. Seconds later, he cleared his throat. "Yeah, Mesha. Hey gurl, it's me. I need you to listen because I have a very important favor to ask you, and it has to stay between you and me. Do you understand me?" He waited. "Good, now listen up. Dis is what I need for you to do."

Chapter 16

"Man, I can't believe you finna trust this silly ass Jamaican. I don't know why, but it feel like we being set up like a muthafucka. Can't you feel it?" Ajani asked. He had an all-black assault rifle on his lap. His finger was already on the trigger. In the back seat was Della, and a big, black heavyset goon that was employed by Ajani's Ski Mask Cartel. He held a pump to the side of Della's head.

"We're both smart enough to know if we're being set up. Just stay on point, and let's do what we gotta do."

I was tired of hearing Ajani complain. He'd been getting on my nerves ever since I'd decided to make a deal with Della.

"Yeah aiight, Joe. If something go wrong, den dis shit on you." He sat back and clutched his rifle firmer.

"Take this road right up here on your left. It's going to lead you into a wooded area. The wooded area will lead you alongside of the Delaware River. Take the road until you start to see the docks. In the docks, you will see a bunch of small boats. The one that your mother is being held on is green. It has a poor paint job. Even in the night like this you will recognize it when you see it."

I nodded. "Cool. Say Della, on some real shit, I apologize for what happened to your brother, man. I know that shit had to cut you deep, but you already know this is how that war shit goes. Unfortunately."

"Yo kid. You apologizin' to dis nigga now and all of dat shit. Fuck is you doing? You don't owe him no fuckin apology," Ajani spat. He looked over his shoulder. "Say nigga, yo brother got what he deserved. Yo punk ass daddy ain't apologized for what he did to my lil cousin, so fuck all of y'all. If it's any foul play going on with this move right here, I'ma send yo ass to dem pearly gates too. Nigga, just so you know."

135

I caught sight of Della's face in the rear view mirror. He looked hateful. His eyebrows were furrowed. He locked eyes with mine and looked off.

"Yo, ain't shit finna go wrong. We finna get my mother back, and that's gone be that. He gon leave with Mesha and everybody is going to live happily ever after," I assured Ajani.

"What about the money?" Della asked.

"What are you talking about?" I looked at him in the rear view mirror again.

"You said that you would send me on my way wit a bag so I could survive for a little while. I'ma need that. After my father finds out your mother has been released, he's going to know it was me who helped to release her. That means he is going to come for me."

"But that's just yo old man. He ain't gon do nothin too serious, right?" Ajani asked.

Della ignored him. "If my father gets ahold of me after I release your mother, he will not only kill me, he will torture me first. He will make an example out of me to this entire country. He will show them what it looks like when anybody crosses him. So, I will need the financial support."

Ajani smacked his lips. "Man, fuck that. Hell n'all. Now you doing way too much. You playin on a ma'fucka's weakness. Nigga, we finna do dis swap. Then we gon go our own separate ways. You be by the best way you know how. It's as simple as that."

Della was silent for a moment before he spoke. "But you gave me your word. You said that hour words were all that we had? What has changed in only a matter of minutes?" Della questioned.

"Nigga, I said what I said," Ajani cut in. He turned around and aimed the assault rifle at Della's forehead. "You got any more questions?"

Della closed his eyes. "I will manage."

I could barely think straight. I was rolling alongside of the Delaware River, right where Derez had been dumped, and I was praying I was getting to my mother in time. There was no way I was going to give Della any money. I wasn't even sure I wasn't going to smoke him after I got my moms back with me. I felt like he was an enemy, and he would always harbor what Ajani did to his brother against the both of us. So, I knew I had to play him real close. "Della, my word is bond," I lied. I got a book bag in the trunk with a hunnit thousand dollars inside of it. It's yours as long as everything goes well. Cool?"

He opened his dark eyes. "Cool."

Ajani shook his head. "You niggas done got soft as hell out here in New York. Fuck this weak ass city now," he snapped. "Soon as we get my Auntie J. back, nigga, you on yo own. You too soft for me."

I ignored him but filed his comments into the back of my brain for later. I wasn't finna let no nigga disrespect me under no circumstances. Ajani might be a killa, but so was I. My body count was just as high as his.

"We're getting closer. Stay on dis road until you get up there where it bends. Then you will see a bunch of row boats. Just to the left of those row boats is a small tunnel that leads to our agreed meeting place."

I nodded and began to follow that path. "Yo sister gon be by herself, right?"

"Of course not. She will more than likely bring security. She doesn't know what she is walking into. Don't be alarmed. You are safe."

"What, nigga? Man, you got us fucked up. Look, I don't give a fuck who she bring. If they want this smoke, they can get it." Ajani cocked his Kay and turned around on high alert.

A strong wind coursed over the car. I had the window rolled down just a tad. It felt good. I was impatient. I wanted my mother back. When I got to the tunnel, I slowed, and rolled inside of it. I took the Uzi out, and set it on my lap driving with my right hand, while I picked the Uzi up with my left, ready to spray.

The tunnel was dark. It smelled like a sewer. The tires echoed on the gravel-like road I was driving down. I clicked on the bright lights and kept rolling. My eyes scanned from left to right over and over. I was almost prepared for a bunch of Jamaicans to jump out at me from every direction. I was fearful of the unknown, but I kept right on rolling.

Ajani rolled down his window and sat on the ledge as if we were getting ready to do a drive by. He tapped his trigger and enacted a red beam. I thought he was out of his mind. I never knew how crazy my cousin news until this night.

After rolling through the tunnel for two full minutes, the road grew slick, and then the path ahead was covered in water. I took my foot off of the gas. "What the fuck is all dat?"

"It happens. It never gets any higher. Just drive," Della said.

I didn't like him giving me orders. It was annoying, and it infuriated me. "Nigga, where the fuck is your sister?"

"Just ahead. You will see a number thirteen, and the tunnel will give you the option of driving either left or right. You'll go left, and she should be parked right there. Our sensors should have already told her we are here."

I remained still for a few moments, trying to think of any angle he could be coming from. If this was a set-up he would of had to be on a suicide mission. There was no way that he could've escaped our custody. Any false moves, and he was getting his head blown off.

"Aiight nigga." I stepped on the gas and followed his directions. It took me five minutes before the tunnel gave me the option to bear either left or right. I chose left. As soon as I made that left, more water was on the road. Then there were a pair of bright fog headlights.

"Up there. There is Mesha up ahead."

I clicked my bright fog lights on and off, signaling for her to do the same, because I was being blinded. She took my cue and cut hers. There she stood, in a fatigue uniform. She held an AK-47 up against her shoulder. To the right of her was my mother. She was being held by a man that looked like he was seven feet tall, with plenty of muscles. In back of him were two more men with long dreads. All of them were in fatigues.

Ajani scanned his red beam off of each man and pinned it straight on Meesha's forehead. "Yo, let my ma'fuckin' auntie go."

My mother squinted. "Ajani, watch yo mouth, boy!"

My heart fluttered. Even in captivity, she was still her. I felt a huge lump form in my throat. She was alive. Words can't even express how I felt to see her standing there alive and well. The only thing that pissed me off was the fact that the built dude was holding her arm all awkward like. I assumed he was hurting her. I threw the car in park. "Keep him. If he do anything stupid, knock his head off," I ordered the shooter that had his pump against the side of Della's head. Then I jumped out of the car and walked right up to the dude holding my mother. I ignored the sounds of the cocking of weapons by his Jamaican shooters.

"Say nigga, why you holding her so tight?" I snapped and slapped at his arm for him to release her. I held my Uzi in my left hand.

He kept his hold. "Orders are orders."

Mesha stepped beside me. "Here is your mother. Now release my brother to our care. A deal is a deal," she said softly. She smelled like Fendi perfume. By the lights of my car I saw she was a beautiful, dark-skinned female. She didn't look any older than nineteen. She was short and well-put together.

"Tell dat nigga to let my mother go right now or we finna have a serious problem," I warned.

Ajani placed his beam on the man's head, and then pulled a .9 out of his waistband, and trained that beam on Mesha's forehead. "Tell him, shorty. Yo time ticking away."

Mesha stepped closer to me. Her lip gloss shimmered in the tunnel. "My brother said you were a man of your word. He said if we gave you your mother, you would release him, and everybody could go their own way. Why are you trying to scam us?" Her voice was soft. She almost spoke in a whisper.

"That nigga got a few seconds to release my mother. Once she's released, then you'll get Della. Now tell him to release her. Now!"

She mugged me. "Do you have any idea what you are getting yourself into? Huh?" She stepped closer. Let my brother up out of that car or feel the wrath of my people."

"Bitch, that's a threat?" Ajani yelled. "Yeah." *Boom. Boom. Boom.*

The dude holding my mother, his face exploded. He flew backward. My mother took off running toward our car. It was like the world stopped. Mesha dropped to the ground. As soon as she did, one of her Jamaican shooters ran beside her. He aimed and fired five shots. *Boom*! *Boom*! *Boom*! *Boom*! *Boom*!

Four of the five bullets ripped into my mother's back and knocked her over the hood of the car. She crashed into it hard, before slumping to the water below.

Ajani chopped him down immediately. His assault rifle jumped in his hands over and over again. The men fell behind me. Mesha jumped up and tried to run away. I don't know what it was. But something made me snap out of it. I reached out, and grabbed a handful of her long dreads, and yanked her back to me. I wrapped my arm around her neck. There was a bright flash inside of the car. Then Della jumped out it and took off running down the tunnel. He disappeared into the darkness. I could hear his footsteps making big splashes in the water.

"Let me go! Let go!" Mesha ordered. Ajani's rifle continued to fire.

"You let them kill her, bitch. This is your fault!" I choked harder.

She beat at my thigh. "Arrgh. Arrgh."

I dragged her back to the car and threw her to Ajani. "Keep this bitch. Damien finna pay for what just happened here."

Ajani nodded. He took her and stuffed her inside of the car. The back door opened. Then he pushed his bodyguard's body out of it. He landed in a pile of water. His head had been blown halfway off.

I knelt to my mother. She squirmed and struggled to breathe. "Huh. Huh. Kaleb. It hurts."

Tears were already coming down my cheeks. I grabbed her into my embrace. Kissed all over her face. "I love you, Mama. Damn. I love you so much, and I tried to get here for you. I tried." I looked into her face. Her eyes were wide open, unblinking. She was slack in my arms. My heart sunk. I cried while holding her. I felt weaker than I ever had in life. I'd lost my entire family. I didn't know what I was going to do, but somebody had to pay. Somebody had to feel the same pain I was feeling.

I kissed her forehead again. Then I slowly lowered her to the water. There was a sewer cap being pulled back a few feet ahead of where our car was parked. A rope came down it.

"Kaleb, let's get the fuck out of here. Come on, man!" Ajani hollered.

I took one last look down to my mother before I rushed to the car. I jumped into the driver's seat. Threw it in reverse and peeled out just as the Jamaicans began to slide down the rope, and into the tunnel heavily armed. I felt lower than dirt.

Chapter 17

"Damn baby, I'm so sorry to hear that," Bree said, the next night as we were parked on Seventh Avenue overlooking Harlem. She rubbed my shoulders. "Are you going to give her a proper burial?"

I shook my head. "I left her back there."

"You what?" she asked in disbelief.

"I had to. Wasn't no sense in bringing her out of there. Besides, how the fuck could I give her a proper funeral? We got so many ma'fuckas looking for us right now, it ain't even funny."

Bree shook her. "Damn and you telling me you wanna bring some babies into this shit? Why?" She removed her hand from me.

I sat in silence. My heart was broken. I was high as a kite and still the pain was crushing my soul. I didn't know what I needed, but I needed something and fast. "I just don't understand it. Why would I be able to get all the way there, only for her to be killed right in front of me?"

Bree sighed. "You want me to be honest with you?"

I looked over to her pretty face. She was without make up. Dark bags were beginning to come under her eyes, but she still looked good. I loved her. "Yeah go ahead."

"From the way you described it to me, and remember, I'm just being uncut. That shit sounded like it was Ajani's fault. Had he not started shooting when he did, our mother would still be alive. At least, that's how it sounds to me."

I stopped to think about it for a minute. I replayed the scene out in my mind play by play. I saw the dude holding my mother. I heard Ajani ordering him to let her go. Then I heard the response in my head from the Jamaican. All of a sudden Ajani was firing. Then my mother was running away from the man that was holding her, before another stepped up and gunned her down. The scene started to play out so vividly in my mind's eye that it felt like I could feel the slugs as they were going into my moms. I jerked and wound up being held by Bree.

"Damn, baby, are you okay?" she asked, holding me tight.

I shook myself out of my zone. "Damn, ma, you're right like a ma'fucka. That nigga did contribute to what happened to her."

"Told you. Now the only thing is, what are you going to do about it?"

I stood up and paced back and forth inside of the hotel. I couldn't think clearly. While it may have been Ajani's fought things had kicked off the way that they had, surely he hadn't done it on purpose. I knew for a fact that he didn't mean for my mother to be shot and killed. "Yo, I'm spacing right now, Bree, if you were me what would you do?"

She stood up and shrugged her shoulders. "Yo daddy, you asking the wrong person. I don't like that nigga no way. He just seem too shiesty to me. So, if I gave you any advice, it would be the wrong, biased advice. I'm just keeping shit real."

That didn't help me at all. I loved my cousin. But sometimes, Ajani could be a total hot head. I felt like I did need to sit him down and get an understanding. But I wasn't sure where that would go. If he said the wrong thing, or reacted in the wrong way, we could potentially wind up trying to kill one another. I didn't wanna go down that road with him. Our family had endured enough murder and tragedy for a lifetime already.

"Yo, you know what, Kaleb? I think you should just holler at him in some man-to-man stuff. Let him know how you feel, and then go from there. But before you do that, you should ask yourself what you are hoping to gain from confronting him about the situation."

I nodded. "Yeah, you right. On some real shit, right now I ain't in a mood to negotiate with nobody. I feel like killing a million ma'fuckas for nothin just because I'm hurting. I can't even think straight."

Bree poked out her bottom lip. "Aw baby, is there anything that I can do for you?" She ran her fingers through her hair and looked as sexy as she could despite how she really was feeling internally.

I looked her up and down. She still looked real good to me. She had on a tank top, with a pair of white lace boy shorts. Her brown thighs were well oiled. Her toes, pretty as usual. "Yo, before I let you know what's really on my mind, you need to tell me how you're feeling about being pregnant again?"

Bree's face grew sour. "Damn, I didn't even wanna think about that right now, Kaleb." She plopped on the bed and crossed her thick thighs.

I came over and sat beside her. I felt like I was getting a cold or something. "I just wanna know, baby? This is important to me."

Bree blew air out of her jaws and lowered her head. "I don't know how to feel, Kaleb. I already told you I'm tired of being down here. I miss Breeyonna, and I feel like I should be with her. She's waiting for me up there."

Not this again, were my first thoughts. I didn't wanna hear about this afterlife talk. I needed to know why she got so down every time we mentioned the fact that she was set to have my seed? "Aiight ma, besides all that?"

"I don't think we got much time left on this earth, Kaleb. I feel like our days are numbered. And even if we do got a nice amount of time, how in the hell are we going to bring a child into our lifestyle?" She sighed dejectedly.

"Why are we thinking so far into the future? When have we ever done that?" I asked, feeling some type of way. I hated how Bree was starting to sound so negative all of the time. We were already faced with so many obstacles, losses, and daily attacks that I simply needed to be able to look to her for some form of positivity. But lately, there had been none that came from her.

"Baby, I just feel how I feel. I can't help the fact that I am going through this, or that I am feeling this way. We've just been through way too much in such a short amount of time. It's bound to get a girl thinking. I've even been thinking on a far worse level than that if you really wanna know."

"Oh yeah? Like what?" She already had me feeling defeated. As much as I loved her, I didn't feel right being around her. My mother's murder was too fresh. Just because I was heartless, didn't mean I was exempt from feeling pain. I was sick over the loss of my mother. Especially because I knew deep down that she'd been murdered because of me. I felt guilty.

Bree got up and started pacing for a moment. She stopped in front of me and took another deep breath. "I feel like us crossing over to each other is the reason why so many of our loved ones are dead. We are solely responsible for the sins that we committed. Instead of Jehovah making us personally pay for our sins. He allowed for the devil to use our loved ones as our sacrifices."

"That don't make no sense Bree. Yo, I swear to God, ever since you OD'ed, you been saying a whole lot of stupid shit. First, you swear up and down that you talked too and saw our deceased loved ones. That Breeyonna told you to come back, and all type of stupid shit. You need to come to grips with the fact that they are gone, and we are still here. It's fucked up, but life has to go on."

"What are you saying, Kaleb? Are you asking me to forget the fact that Buddy's bitch ass did what he did to my daughter, and the reason he did it is because we fucked around behind his back? Huh? You think I shouldn't be woman enough to admit that I am fifty percent of the reason my little girl is gone right now? Huh?" She stepped closer, until she was standing right in front of me.

I stood up and looked down on her. "Nah shorty, I ain't saying none of that. All I'm saying is that it's time we move forward with our lives. We gotta salvage out shit while we still have it. Us having a baby could be a good thing. It means we have a new life to protect, which means that we are going to be forced to leave this street life alone. That's all I'm saying." I held her arms. "Bree, I love you with all of my heart. I wanna be with you for the rest of my life, I don't care how long, or how short that I have left. I want you to have our child. I want us to be a family. I think after so much heartache and pain, we deserve some happiness. Why can't we escape this world of darkness together? Why can't we roll off into the sunset holding each other down in unconditional love?"

She shook her head. "Because we can't. We've commuted too much wrong. Karma is coming for us. Then on top of that my heart is black, Kaleb. I'm afraid to love. I'm afraid to believe that we will be anything other than hurt. I can't take what's going on inside of me. That's why I asked you to kill me. I need you to take me out of this pain and misery." She fell against me. She stayed there for a second, then pushed me away, and turned her back to me. "I wanna hear you say it."

I stepped behind her, and wrapped my arms around her protectively. My heart was hurting me. I kept seeing my mother's face. Then Derez's. Then Destiny's. Rayven's and lastly, but not less painful, Breeyonna's. "What, baby? Talk to me."

She sniffled. "I wanna hear you say that us crossing over to one another was a bad idea. That we are the reason that so many have died. That our union was selfish, and toxic."

"Never. I been in love with you from day-one. All I've ever saw was you, Bree. And I'm a street nigga, but even street niggas fall in love with that one special female. It's always been you. It's just that you were with Buddy. But even still, I couldn't help jocking you from the corners of my eyes whenever you were in the room."

"That makes you disloyal. You was supposed to be loyal to Buddy. You were never supposed to pursue me. How the fuck could I trust you when your own right-hand man couldn't even do that when you were supposed to be his better half in those slums? You ain't right, Kaleb. You know you ain't right."

"I don't give a fuck. I had to have you. If I had to do it all over again, I would. I would because I know that you are who I am supposed to be with." I spun her around. "Look, I know we may have not made the right decisions. I know we may have went about things the wrong way, but I love you. I can't help the way I feel. I wish I could. I can't live in regrets. That ain't gon get us nowhere. All we have is today. All we have is each other. And I'ma fight for you, Bree. I'm fight for you until a ma'fucka take me out of the game. Believe that."

She sniffled and allowed for me to wipe her tears away with my thumbs. "But why, Kaleb? Why do you love me so much? I can't benefit you the way another woman could have. I didn't have anything to offer. Rayven was the total package. What would make you choose me over her? What would make you fuck out lives up like this?"

I shrugged my shoulders. "I don't know. I really don't have all of the answers. All I know is that I wasn't gon take the easy road out. I didn't want nothing handed to me. I wanted to fight for you because anything worst having, and cherishing is worth fighting for until the death. You are worth my fight, Bree. Even with all of the losses, and all of the deaths. I still choose you. I will always choose you. Just stop making me feel like a damn fool for doing so."

She shook her head slowly. "I can't Kaleb. I can't do this right now. I'm still not strong enough." She fell to her knees. Her small hands covered her face. "I'm hurting so bad. Oh, why did God take Breeyonna? Why did I do that to my little cousin? Who cares if she was only related to me through marriage. I should've never killed her in that cornfield. She was just a kid. I hate myself so bad." She started to break down real badly, rocking back and forth.

I wrapped her in my arms and held her while she cried. "Life happens, Bree. We can't do nothing but play the cards we were dealt. But I'm letting you know right now that I ain't going nowhere. If we gon sit here on this floor and cry all night together, then that's just what we gon do. As long as in the end, we come up with a plan for you to be with me, along with our child, then we can leave this street life alone, and sail off into the sunset."

Bree was quiet for a long time. She just kept hugging me tighter and tighter. "Kaleb, I need you to hold me all night. I need you to hold me and tell me that everything is going to be okay. Please. Heal me and make me your woman all over again. I am better than this. We are better than this."

"I got you, boo. I promise." We climbed in the bed and held each other while we cried until the emotional pain started to hurt less and less. Finally, after three hours of endless tears, and opening up to each other, we drifted off to sleep, weak, but united and stronger as one.

Chapter 18

When I woke up the next morning, Bree was standing over me with a smile on her face. Her hair looked like she'd recently got it done. The curls were popping and seemed full of sheen. I could smell a subtle scent of perfume coming off of her. She turned her head sideways. "Dang, are you woke yet? What, you plan on sleeping the whole freaking day away?"

I scooted to the top of the bed and rested my back against the pillows. Yawned, and stretched my arms above my head. "How long you been woke?"

"Long enough to go and grab this." She reached down and picked up a suitcase from the side of the bed. She tossed it on to the comforter and unzipped it. Before she opened it to my sight, she smiled at me. "I never want you to underestimate me, Kaleb." She pulled it open and revealed the contents inside.

I frowned and looked into the opening at stacks upon stacks of cash. It looked like it had to be every bit of four to five hundred thousand dollars. "Where did you get all of this money from?"

"I been had it. Well, actually Buddy did. But when all of this shit hit the fan, I hit his stash that he didn't know I knew he had. Sho did." She ran her fingers through the bills. "Dat muthafucka took my daughter away from me, Kaleb. And I know that deep down, me taking this money had somethin to do with it. So, you see, I haven't been as upfront with you as I should have been." Her smile turned into look of sorrow. Bree seemed bipolar to me.

I scooted out of the bed and looked the money over closely. "Wait a minute. You got this from Buddy? How much is it?"

"Seven hundred thousand dollars. It's just enough for us to start our life anew. I'm choosing you, Kaleb. I know that Bree wants me to come back to her, but I can't. I have to choose you. I want to live the best life that I can, no matter how short of it may be. The pain of her death still haunts me every second of every day, but still in all, I have to be strong. We deserve to give this baby that I am carrying a chance."

I was still stunned with the whole money thing. "Baby, all that sounds good. But when were you able to get this money from Buddy?"

"When he got locked up in New Jersey the first time, I heard him talking on the phone to one of his lil guys. He suspected that you and I were fuckin around for a long time. He was saying that he was going to do a little more digging before he took both of us out of the game. I knew that he was going to make a move on us, but I didn't know how soon. However, I wanted to leave him. But I couldn't leave empty-handed. I knew I would never be able to take care of Breeyonna on my own. The financial responsibility would have been too much. I was scared. So, I watched him closely. One day when he nodded out on that heroin shit, he left the safe wide open. I looked inside and I saw all of this. For the next few days afterwards, whenever he wasn't in the house I tried different combinations until I cracked his code. Long story short. There is the money that is going to start our life anew."

My mind was racing. "But Buddy made it seem like his hatred was because you and I had betrayed him. He ain't never say shit about no money. Why wouldn't he ever bring it up?"

"Pride. Damn Kaleb, are you that fuckin naive?" She shook her head and ran her fingers through her hair. "You already took me from his ass. Was fucking me while you and he were right-hand men. Then to top it off, I took his whole stash, and for all he knew I brought it to you. That's a double whammy. I don't know no real nigga in these slums that would admit some shit like that. Instead of admitting what really happened, he chose to go berserk. Now that you know everything, can you blame him?"

I was blown away. I had already been the reason that Buddy's hand had been cut off. While bussing a move for one of the heavy hittas in New York, I'd pinched a few gees from the stash in order to help my mother pay for her medications. Buddy had been suspected, and because he had they had cut his hand off. On top of that, because of me, more than a few crews in New York had been at our throats, including the Jamaicans. Through it all, Buddy attempted to ride by my side, one hunnit. Not knowing that I was fucking the love of his life behind his back. Fucking and falling in love with her. Yeah, I guess now that I thought about it, we had fucked him over in an ugly way.

"Now you see it. I can tell by the look in your eyes." She sat on the bed. "What are we going to do?" She looked over to me.

"Ain't shit we can do. We gotta get the fuck out of New York. I'm talking like the first thing in the morning. I gotta empty out two of the three accounts that Rayven set up for me. I pray they will let me. It's only a matter of time before the police are on our ass. We need to travel with cash. It's a combined total eight hundred thousand put up. That money should help us to live free for a little while. But if them people get on our ass they gon lock those accounts, and we gon be fucked."

"So, what are you saying?" Bree asked, standing up.

"I'm saying we gotta get out of here as soon as we can. We can't win this war. Karma is against us."

"That's what I thought. Now you got me scared." She zipped the suitcase and sat back beside it. "What about

Destiny. You gotta get her back from Buddy. How are you going to do that?"

Bomp. Bomp. Bomp. Bomp.

Reflexes made me grab both .40 Glocks out of the small of my back. I rushed to the door and waved for Bree to go into the bathroom. "Get into the tub in case I gotta start bucking." When she closed the door behind her, I turned back to the door. "Who is it?"

"Ajani, cuz, open up."

The beats of my heart slowed. I sighed in relief. When I opened the door, Ajani mugged me. "Fuck you looking at me all crazy for?" I asked him, stepping away.

"You can't answer your phone a somethin?" He closed the door and stepped further into the room. Spotted the suitcase. "Sure, y'all going?"

I followed his eyes and waved the suitcase off. "Aw that ain't what you think it is." I grabbed my phone from the dresser and turned it back on. "And I had my phone off, because me and Bree was going through something last night. I needed to be fully focused on her." I went to the bathroom and knocked on the door after seeing it was locked. "Baby, it's good. It's just my cousin Ajani." I waited for Bree to come to the door so she could unlock it from the inside.

"Damn nigga, who the fuck you done robbed?" Ajani asked. When I turned around I saw that he had the suitcase unzipped and looking over the bills. He zipped it back up.

"Damn nigga, yo nosey ass. Get the fuck out of our shit," I snapped, grabbing the suitcase off of the bed. I set it on the floor.

"Excuse me." He placed his hands in the air.

Bree came out of the bathroom and stepped next to me. "What is he doing here?"

"Aw, here we go with this shit. Shawty, I thought we squashed all that bullshit a lil while ago?" Ajani got up and pulled a bottled water from his coat pocket.

"I ain't got nothing to say to you. But stay out of my shit." She rolled her eyes and popped her neck. Grabbed the suitcase off of the floor. Then sat on the bed, hugging it.

Ajani mugged her for a minute, then shook his head. "See, Dat's what a ma'fucka get when he try his best to be respectful to dese hoez."

"Yo, chill nigga. I done already told you what it was when it came to her. Respect my baby, Kid. Word up," I said, getting heated by the minute.

Ajani waved her off. "Fuck that. Look, I got the drop on that nigga Damien. Remember I was telling you that my brother Rayjon would follow me over here from Chicago?"

I nodded. "Yeah, what about it?"

"Dat nigga Rayjon got a baby by a bitch whose brother works for Damien as one of his top security men. Anyway, we know where that nigga gone be laying his head tonight. I wanna take Mesha over there, and whack her pops in front of her for what they did to Auntie J. The only thing is we gotta move like right now. Damien just got back from Kingston. He taking a load off in the Hamptons. Can you believe that shit?"

I couldn't. I shook my head and looked over to Bree. "Look Ajani, I gotta take like eight hundred racks out of the bank as soon as possible. I'ma add it with Bree's money, and we gon get the fuck up out of New York before the feds get involved. That's if they ain't already got involved. But I need to get this money out like right away. Then we can go hit Damien and go from there."

"Wait a minute. Eight hundred racks, where y'all finna go with all of that money, cuz?" Ajani questioned.

"Anywhere but New York. Shit, we gotta leave the East Coast period. We need to hit up one of those islands with no extradition," Bree added.

Ajani sighed. "Damn nigga. We was just getting to know each other. Maybe y'all should come down to Chicago. We done built a nice lil life for us down there. The family got that city on lock."

"Hard pass. Only people that make it in Chicago is the people that are born there. We need to go somewhere tropical. Right, daddy? We gotta give dis one a chance." Bree rubbed her stomach.

"And you pregnant?" Ajani acted like his mind was blown. "Yo dis shit wild. Anyway, go do what you gotta do. I'll be back to scoop you up in four hours. That should be enough time."

I gave him a half-hug and gripped the back of his head Harlem style. "Sound like a plan."

***

Bree's eyes looked like they wanted to pop out of her face. "Baby, I never seen this much money before. Look how it's spilling out of both suitcases," she said, pointing at the two Burberry suitcases stuffed with cash. I still can't believe they gave it to you without giving you much of a hassle."

"Aw, they gave me a hassle. Since I needed it so urgently, they made me pay a serious fee of thirty thousand dollars. Had I not paid it, they would have made me wait for seventy-two hours."

Thirty gees? Are you serious? They got over big time." Bree said. She looked disappointed in me. "Do you really think it was that serious?"

"We got the money, don't we?"

She nodded. "I guess."

She sat on the bed, and opened a box of pizza she'd ordered and picked up. "Baby, do you think we'll make it?"

I nodded. "Yeah, we ain't got no other choice but to."

She laughed and stopped abruptly, once again showing me signs of her bipolar defect. "Would you be mad at me if I told you I was scared?" She climbed into the bed

I shook my head. "Nope. We been through a lot. We got a whole bunch of enemies. Only God knows what the future might bring." I set the suitcases beside one another on the floor, then climbed into the bed beside Bree. She laid on her side. I wanted to feel that big ass in my lap. I hugged up to her.

"Daddy, why didn't you ever come down on me for stealing Buddy's money? You know you were supposed to. Who's to say that all of this isn't my fault?"

I rested my face in her hair. She smelled good. I had always loved the smell of Bree. "Ain't no sense in me making you feel worse than you already feel. You should know that you fucked up by hitting that nigga. But still in all, he should've took that shit out on us, not our babies. Second to that, I pursued you, so whatever you did to fuck that nigga over, I'm just as guilty as you are. I ain't got no room to be pointing fingers."

"Yeah, I know but..." She sighed. "Well, I guess the reason I feel so bad is because I honestly think I am the cause of my daughter's murder. If you tried to live with that guilt every single day, it would eventually kill you. I should be punished. I just don't know how."

I adjusted myself behind her and grabbed a handful of her hair roughly. Yanked her head back. "It's been a while. I know how." I yanked up her nightgown and ripped her panties from her frame with the exception of one of the leg hole that got caught around her thigh. My piece sprang out.

"Not right now, Kaleb. Please, daddy. My head is screwed up." She fought against me.

I picked her lil ass up and slammed her to the bed. Then I was on top of her. She bucked upward to try and get me off of her. The more she fought, the more excited I became. I had to have Bree. Since day-one, she did somethin to me. I felt like this woman was my apple. My sin that would cause so much death, yet I had to take as many bites of her as I could. And even when my mouth was full, I kept on biting more and more of her until her juices were running down my chin.

"Uhhhh!" she moaned.

I found her sex lips wet. Slipped inside of her and proceed to beat her walls loose. She breathe heavy against my neck. Her nails dug into my sides. "Dis my pussy. Uh. Uh. I need this pussy, Bree." Faster, and harder. Deeper. "I need you."

She humped into me, fuckin back. "Aw. Aw. Why? Why? Shit! Why?" Her legs wrapped around my waist while I pounded her out like a maniac.

"You. Belong. To. Me." Faster, and faster I dove. Her box felt hotter. Tighter than usual. I couldn't hold back. I felt her sucking on my neck. When she added teeth, I came, growling like an angry lion.

It must've triggered hers, because the next thing I knew she screamed loud. Dug her nails into me even deeper and scratched. She came, jerking underneath me, shaking uncontrollably, before she collapsed on her back crying. "I'm so sorry for getting us into this mess. It's all my fault. I'm so, so sorry, Breeyonna." She pulled me down on top of her. "Hold me, Kaleb. Please. Just keep holding me until you have to leave tonight."

I did. I didn't understand how she could be up one minute, and then the next she was down like a power line. I knew she was going through some serious emotional and mental battles, but I didn't know what to do to help her other than to hold her like she requested.

T.J. Edwards

Chapter 19

I followed Ajani's lead as he crept through the sliding back patio door. Behind us was a swimming pool that looked like it belonged indoors. It was huge. There was a slide attached to it, and two diving boards. On the way to the back door I spotted a tennis court, and three four-wheelers. Damien's bitch ass was definitely living lavish. The Underworld had treated him real well.

Both me and Ajani were dressed in all black, with black ski masks, and black Timbs. Even my leather gloves were black. I didn't know what to expect. We were dealing with a Jamaican that had a lot of pull and prestige that reported all the way back to Jamaica. All Ajani kept telling me was that he had everything under control. To trust him. So, I did.

We eased inside and stepped directly into the kitchen. It was also massive. A big white refrigerator. A stove that looked like five people could cook on it at once. The floors were marble. There was a ceiling fan on low that kept the breeze flowing.

Ajani pointed toward the hallway and waved me to follow. My heart was pounding in my chest. I felt like I couldn't breathe easily. I had a cold that made the left side of my face feel like it was stopped up. A sore throat. All of it was fucking with my mental. I tried to shake it off and focus but for some reason, my brain felt cloudy. I didn't know what I was walking into. I was used to being the leader and now I was forced to follow my cousin.

The house was dark. When we got to the hallway, he crept down it and ducked low. I followed suit. For a wealthy man, I was surprised that he didn't have bodyguards all over the place. Something about that seemed so unnatural to me. Ajani kept going. He took the hallway all the way to the end and turned down on to another short one. This one had three doors. There was light coming from under only one of the doors. Before we could make it to that one, it opened. Rayjon stepped into the hallway with a black winter mask covering only half of his face. "Fuck took y'all so long? I done did every fuckin thang already." He stepped back into the room.

I stood all the way up. My heart was still pounding. Ajani walked into the room ahead of me. When I stepped inside of it my breath was taken away. The room was huge. Rayjon had Damien and Mesha tied to chairs with socks in their mouths. He made them face one another. Also, in the room were six of his Ski Mask Cartel killas.

Ajani nodded his head. "Awright big bro. Dis how you handle that ma'fuckin' bidness den." Ajani hugged his older brother.

Rayjon broke the embrace and stood in front of Damien. "So dis bitch ass nigga was responsible for killing my lil cousin and my auntie, right?"

Ajani nodded. "Hell yeah. Fuck nigga been giving us problems since before I even came out here."

"Well, unlucky for him, the Ski Mask Cartel is here." Rayjon knelt down and dug his hand into a black medical bag. He pulled out a small scalpel and looked over his shoulder at me. "Lil cuz, I'm sorry for our losses. I wish I would of some out here sooner, but I was conducting some political bidness for the family." He looked down to Damien. "We finna make his ass pay though. Ajani, make sure this bitch is watching the whole time. If she closes her eyes, you rock her ass. That's an order."

"I got you, bruh." He grabbed Mesha by the head and held her steady. "Watch this, shawty. You ain't gon wanna miss a beat."

"Yo, Stop me at any time you wanna take over, Kaleb. I'm just gone get him prime and ready for you. You see, the Ski Mask Cartel is spreading out to Jamaica, and a few other islands, but in order to do so we gotta go through this bitch ass nigga, and them punk ass Vega's out here in New York and Cuba. This nigga finna be the first down. Yo, Mac, make sure younger this shit on camera." One of his bodyguards pulled out a phone and began recording. "Dis to all you drug lords alike. The Ski Mask Cartel is coming for you bitches." He pulled the sock out of Damien's mouth. "Cry for our life bitch."

Damien remained silent. "I love you, Mesha."

Rayjon pulled his hand back and slammed the scalpel into Damien's cheek. He pulled it downward and ripped it to the left, then the right. Blood spurt into the air like a fire hydrant.

Ajani laughed and continued to hold Mesha's face steady. "Dat's what the fuck I'm talking 'bout. We coming fa dese niggas, man."

Rayjon slammed the scalpel into his forehead, dragged it downward. He split his lip in two. Damien jerked, then he started to groan under his breath.

"Nall, kid, you wanna really hurt a nigga, you gotta torture his baby girl in front of him." Ajani stepped in front of Mesha. He knelt down and grabbed a hammer out of Rayjon's black bag. He stood up and laughed out loud. He pointed the hammer at the camera. "The world is ours." He swung it and slammed it into Mesha's temple, caving it in. She slumped forward with the hammer still inside of her.

"Noooo!" Damien hollered.

Rayjon punched him in the mouth. Took the scalpel and sliced him back and forth over and over again. By the time he stood back Damien's face was unrecognizable. Blood dripped all around his chair. Rayjon snatched his Jamaican piece from around his neck and held it up for the camera. "Jamaica belongs to the Ski Mask Cartel."

Ajani had beat Mesha's head in so bad that it had caved inward. He kicked her chair over. "I'm the muthafuckin king of New York. You hear me, Vegas? Huh, Tristian, or bitch ass Showbiz?"

I didn't know who they were talking about, but obviously this shit was bigger than me. I didn't know what to do or to say. Rayjon stepped up to me and handed me a military knife. "Do the honors, Kaleb. End this nigga for what he did to our family."

Damien blinked with blood dripping off of him. His entire face was covered in blood. It looked like he had a red plastic mask on. "Long live Jamaica. Della will avenge me." He spit blood at Rayjon just as I raised the knife.

Rayjon wiped his face. Came off of his waist with a .40 caliber and slammed it into Damien's right eye, before blowing that whole side of his face off with four bullets. Damien dropped to the ground. Rayjon stomped him until the entire room was covered in blood. It was the most gruesome scene that I had ever witnessed.

***

While we rolled through New York some time later that night, Ajani, couldn't help snickering. "Yo, you seem like you fucked up in the head."

"You niggas went crazy, B. The shit didn't seem like it had nothin to do with the death of my moms, or brother at all. What did y'all really have against Damien?"

Ajani dumped a bit of China White onto the back of his hand and tooted it off. He pinched his nostrils until I guess the feeling began to course through him. "Dis shit bigger than what you got going on, Kaleb. What we just did back there was street justice for what that nigga people did to our blood-line, but at the same time we are forced to beat any major mob-ster in the game right now. Our Cartel is about to be bigger than El Chapo's Sinaloa Cartel."

"What?" I didn't even know what the fuck he was talking about.

"We on bidness, and ma'fuckas gotta do what they gotta do to move full steam ahead. Rayjon is in the King spots and I'm just a lil bit under him. We putting on for the memory of my pops Greed, and my mother Jersey. They died so we could live like true kings."

I nodded. "Right."

Damien was in the way. Just like the Vegas out here in the way, and them niggas that call themselves the Coke Kings over there in Harlem. Right now, it's a war going on in the narcotics world that ain't no Cartel safe from. We eating these niggas like cannibals," he hissed. "The Ski Mask Cartel in the end will run this world. And what's crazy is that very few ma'fuckas even know that I'm alive. According to the game, I'm already dead. But sometimes you gotta fake yo death until you can be resurrected as a king. God sold me another life and made a prophet." He closed his eyes and nodded. "The world is ours, nigga, just stay tuned."

I pulled the car to the curb of the hotel and parked it. "Yo, I still don't understand what you niggas really got going on, but all I can do is wish you the best. I appreciate y'all handling dude bitch ass for me. I needed that assistance."

"Come on, cuz, say no more. On some real shit, I already know that I'm partially to blame for what happened wit Auntie. I should've bucked that nigga down before he had the chance to shoot her. But I slept and because I did, she lost her life. However, in a matter of months, I'ma have a million dollars for you and a lil property on the island of Cuba. The Cartel moving through these islands, bruh. We living like kings already, but it's only the beginning. First it's the takeover, and then we live good. There is still place for you, long as you turn your killa up."

"I'll get back to you on that, for now I need to get in here and come up with a plan with Bree. Yo, I love you, kid." I hugged him.

"I love you too, Joe. Next up is Buddy's ass. We gon catch him before we leave for Havana. That's my word." He kissed my cheek.

***

When I stepped inside of the hotel, Bree was sitting on the bed, listening to Ella Mae's "Naked" song. She looked up to me with mascara running down her cheeks. She had a thirty-eight Special in her hand. It had a silencer on the end of it. There were bullets all over the bed. I closed the door and eased into the room. The blinds were closed, but she had one lamp on. It illuminated the room just enough. "Baby, what's the matter?"

"Today is Breeyonna's birthday." She sniffled.

I looked down at the floor and saw she had all of our suitcases packed, and on the side of the bed. "Okay, baby, well, let's celebrate her the right way, not like this."

Bree placed four bullets in the chamber and closed the cylinder. She put the barrel of the gun to her temple and cocked the hammer. "It's my fault that he killed her, Kaleb. It's my fault that he did all of this. I can't take this pain anymore." Tears ran down her face.

"Bree calm down, ma, damn. I thought we already been over this?" I said irritated.

166

She slowly shook her head. "Kaleb, I love you, but we can't fight karma. We can't get away with what we did without paying the consequences."

"What the fuck are you talking about? Are you losing your mind or something?"

"With karma, it's all about sacrifice. In order for me and Breeyonna to be reunited in heaven, I have no other choice other than to make a deal with God. I have to kill the devil. I have too," she insisted.

"Bree, you are tripping. What the fuck is wrong with you?"

"There are many forms of the devil. I have to be with Breeyonna. I sent her there. I have to protect her from here on out. I can't go up to be with her, so I gotta bring her back down with me." Bree squeezed out more tears.

Now I was heated. "Bree, snap out of that shit. Now! We gotta move on. We gon start again with the one in your stomach. You can't bring Breeyonna back. It's impossible."

"She's already here. She came back and you just didn't know it. I had to make a deal with him, Kaleb. I'm sorry." Before I could even process what she was saying, she aimed the .38 at me and fired.

The slug smacked into my chest and sent me falling backward into the dresser. The bullet burned through me. It felt like it had torn a chunk out of my lungs. I couldn't breathe. I sunk to the floor. My throat filled with blood.

Bree stood over me. She looked down with a sinister expression on her face. You started this, Kaleb. You should've never came for me. We would never be here."

I felt weak. I struggled to get up. I used the dresser. When I was almost at a standstill, she fired another slug knocking the right side of my jaw off. I fell onto my back, still looking up to her.

Buddy stepped out of the bathroom and slid his arm around her waist. In his left arm was Destiny. He kissed my daughter on the forehead. She cried. He bounced her up and down. "Shush, Breeyonna. It's okay. Daddy right here. Its gon be okay. Gon head and finish him, baby. Only then can Breeyonna's soul fully enter into this child of God. His death will make her rise up to His power," he whispered.

Bree stood over me with the gun. "I'm sorry, Kaleb. I never meant for any of this to happen. I swear to God I will always love you." She aimed and fired another shot to my chest. My eyes bucked wide open. I was frozen still. I could feel my blood pouring out of me.

Buddy laughed. He threw Destiny to the floor like a football after a touchdown and slammed his gun to the back of Bree's head. "Bitch ain't never been right." *Boom*!

She fell on top of me shaking, her noodles seeping out of her. Buddy laughed. He filled her with five more slugs, then pulled her off of me. He knelt down. "Karma's a bitch nigga named Buddy, huh." He aimed and finger fucked his gun.

To Be Continued. . .
Rise to Power 4
Coming Soon

Submission Guideline

Submit the first three chapters of your completed manuscript to ldpsubmissions@gmail.com, subject line: Your book's title. The manuscript must be in a .doc file and sent as an attachment. Document should be in Times New Roman, double spaced and in size 12 font. Also, provide your synopsis and full contact information. If sending multiple submissions, they must each be in a separate email.

Have a story but no way to send it electronically? You can still submit to LDP/Ca$h Presents. Send in the first three chapters, written or typed, of your completed manuscript to:

LDP: Submissions Dept
Po Box 870494
Mesquite, Tx 75187

DO NOT send original manuscript. Must be a duplicate.

Provide your synopsis and a cover letter containing your full contact information.

Thanks for considering LDP and Ca$h Presents.

Coming Soon from Lock Down Publications/Ca$h Presents

BOW DOWN TO MY GANGSTA

By **Ca$h**

TORN BETWEEN TWO

By **Coffee**

BLOOD STAINS OF A SHOTTA **III**

By **Jamaica**

STEADY MOBBIN **III**

By **Marcellus Allen**

BLOOD OF A BOSS **VI**

SHADOWS OF THE GAME II

By **Askari**

LOYAL TO THE GAME **IV**

By **T.J. & Jelissa**

A DOPEBOY'S PRAYER **II**

By **Eddie "Wolf" Lee**

IF LOVING YOU IS WRONG… **III**

By **Jelissa**

TRUE SAVAGE **VII**

MIDNIGHT CARTEL

DOPE BOY MAGIC

By **Chris Green**

BLAST FOR ME **III**

DUFFLE BAG CARTEL **IV**

HEARTLESS GOON **II**

By **Ghost**

A HUSTLER'S DECEIT III

KILL ZONE **II**

BAE BELONGS TO ME III

SOUL OF A MONSTER III

By **Aryanna**

THE COST OF LOYALTY **III**

By **Kweli**

THE SAVAGE LIFE II

By **J-Blunt**

KING OF NEW YORK V

COKE KINGS IV

BORN HEARTLESS II

By **T.J. Edwards**

GORILLAZ IN THE BAY IV

De'Kari

THE STREETS ARE CALLING II

Duquie Wilson

KINGPIN KILLAZ IV

STREET KINGS III

PAID IN BLOOD III

CARTEL KILLAZ II

Hood Rich

SINS OF A HUSTLA II

ASAD

TRIGGADALE III

Elijah R. Freeman

KINGZ OF THE GAME IV

Playa Ray

SLAUGHTER GANG IV

RUTHLESS HEART II

By Willie Slaughter

THE HEART OF A SAVAGE II

By Jibril Williams

FUK SHYT II

By Blakk Diamond

THE DOPEMAN'S BODYGAURD II

By Tranay Adams

TRAP GOD II

By Troublesome

YAYO II

A SHOOTER'S AMBITION

By S. Allen

GHOST MOB

Stilloan Robinson

KINGPIN DREAMS

By Paper Boi Rari

CREAM

By Yolanda Moore

SON OF A DOPE FIEND II

By Renta

FOREVER GANGSTA

By Adrian Dulan

LOYALTY AIN'T PROMISED

By Keith Williams

THE PRICE YOU PAY FOR LOVE
By Destiny Skai
THE LIFE OF A HOOD STAR
By Rashia Wilson

<u>Available Now</u>

RESTRAINING ORDER **I & II**
By **CA$H & Coffee**
LOVE KNOWS NO BOUNDARIES **I II & III**
By **Coffee**
RAISED AS A GOON I, II, III & IV
BRED BY THE SLUMS I, II, III
BLAST FOR ME I & II
ROTTEN TO THE CORE I II III
A BRONX TALE I, II, III
DUFFEL BAG CARTEL I II III
HEARTLESS GOON
A SAVAGE DOPEBOY
HEARTLESS GOON
By **Ghost**
LAY IT DOWN **I & II**
LAST OF A DYING BREED
BLOOD STAINS OF A SHOTTA I & II
By **Jamaica**
LOYAL TO THE GAME
LOYAL TO THE GAME II

LOYAL TO THE GAME III

LIFE OF SIN I, II III

By **TJ & Jelissa**

BLOODY COMMAS I & II

SKI MASK CARTEL I II & III

KING OF NEW YORK I II,III IV

RISE TO POWER I II III

COKE KINGS I II III

BORN HEARTLESS

By **T.J. Edwards**

IF LOVING HIM IS WRONG…I & II

LOVE ME EVEN WHEN IT HURTS I II III

By **Jelissa**

WHEN THE STREETS CLAP BACK I & II III

By **Jibril Williams**

A DISTINGUISHED THUG STOLE MY HEART I II & III

LOVE SHOULDN'T HURT I II III IV

RENEGADE BOYS I II III IV

By **Meesha**

A GANGSTER'S CODE I &, II III

A GANGSTER'S SYN I II III

THE SAVAGE LIFE

By **J-Blunt**

PUSH IT TO THE LIMIT

By **Bre' Hayes**

BLOOD OF A BOSS **I, II, III, IV, V**

SHADOWS OF THE GAME

By **Askari**

THE STREETS BLEED MURDER **I, II & III**

THE HEART OF A GANGSTA I II& III

By **Jerry Jackson**

CUM FOR ME

CUM FOR ME 2

CUM FOR ME 3

CUM FOR ME 4

CUM FOR ME 5

An **LDP Erotica Collaboration**

BRIDE OF A HUSTLA **I II & II**

THE FETTI GIRLS **I, II& III**

CORRUPTED BY A GANGSTA I, II III, IV

BLINDED BY HIS LOVE

By **Destiny Skai**

WHEN A GOOD GIRL GOES BAD

By **Adrienne**

THE COST OF LOYALTY I II

By Kweli

A GANGSTER'S REVENGE **I II III & IV**

THE BOSS MAN'S DAUGHTERS

THE BOSS MAN'S DAUGHTERS II

THE BOSSMAN'S DAUGHTERS III

THE BOSSMAN'S DAUGHTERS IV

THE BOSS MAN'S DAUGHTERS **V**

A SAVAGE LOVE **I & II**

BAE BELONGS TO ME I II

A HUSTLER'S DECEIT I, II, III

WHAT BAD BITCHES DO I, II, III

SOUL OF A MONSTER I II

KILL ZONE

By **Aryanna**

A KINGPIN'S AMBITON

A KINGPIN'S AMBITION **II**

I MURDER FOR THE DOUGH

By **Ambitious**

TRUE SAVAGE

TRUE SAVAGE II

TRUE SAVAGE **III**

TRUE SAVAGE **IV**

TRUE SAVAGE **V**

TRUE SAVAGE **VI**

By **Chris Green**

A DOPEBOY'S PRAYER

By **Eddie "Wolf" Lee**

THE KING CARTEL **I, II & III**

By **Frank Gresham**

THESE NIGGAS AIN'T LOYAL **I, II & III**

By **Nikki Tee**

GANGSTA SHYT **I II &III**

By **CATO**

THE ULTIMATE BETRAYAL

By **Phoenix**

BOSS'N UP **I , II & III**

By **Royal Nicole**

I LOVE YOU TO DEATH

By Destiny J

I RIDE FOR MY HITTA

I STILL RIDE FOR MY HITTA

By **Misty Holt**

LOVE & CHASIN' PAPER

By **Qay Crockett**

TO DIE IN VAIN

SINS OF A HUSTLA

By **ASAD**

BROOKLYN HUSTLAZ

By **Boogsy Morina**

BROOKLYN ON LOCK I & II

By **Sonovia**

GANGSTA CITY

By **Teddy Duke**

A DRUG KING AND HIS DIAMOND I & II III

A DOPEMAN'S RICHES

HER MAN, MINE'S TOO I, II

CASH MONEY HO'S

By Nicole Goosby

TRAPHOUSE KING **I II & III**

KINGPIN KILLAZ I II III

STREET KINGS I II

PAID IN BLOOD **I II**

CARTEL KILLAZ

T.J. Edwards

By **Hood Rich**

LIPSTICK KILLAH **I, II, III**

CRIME OF PASSION I & II

By **Mimi**

STEADY MOBBN' **I, II, III**

By **Marcellus Allen**

WHO SHOT YA **I, II, III**

SON OF A DOPE FIEND

Renta

GORILLAZ IN THE BAY **I II III**

DE'KARI

TRIGGADALE I II

Elijah R. Freeman

GOD BLESS THE TRAPPERS I, II, III

THESE SCANDALOUS STREETS I, II, III

FEAR MY GANGSTA I, II, III

THESE STREETS DON'T LOVE NOBODY I, II

BURY ME A G I, II, III, IV, V

A GANGSTA'S EMPIRE I, II, III, IV

THE DOPEMAN'S BODYGAURD

Tranay Adams

THE STREETS ARE CALLING

Duquie Wilson

MARRIED TO A BOSS... I II III

By **Destiny Skai & Chris Green**

KINGZ OF THE GAME I II III

Playa Ray

SLAUGHTER GANG I II III

RUTHLESS HEART

By Willie Slaughter

THE HEART OF A SAVAGE

By Jibril Williams

FUK SHYT

By Blakk Diamond

DON'T F#CK WITH MY HEART I II

By Linnea

ADDICTED TO THE DRAMA I II III

By Jamila

YAYO

By S. Allen

TRAP GOD

By Troublesome

<u>BOOKS BY LDP'S CEO, CA$H</u>

<u>TRUST IN NO MAN</u>

<u>TRUST IN NO MAN 2</u>

<u>TRUST IN NO MAN 3</u>

<u>BONDED BY BLOOD</u>

<u>SHORTY GOT A THUG</u>

<u>THUGS CRY</u>

<u>THUGS CRY 2</u>

<u>THUGS CRY 3</u>

<u>TRUST NO BITCH</u>

<u>TRUST NO BITCH 2</u>

<u>TRUST NO BITCH 3</u>

<u>TIL MY CASKET DROPS</u>

<u>RESTRAINING ORDER</u>

<u>RESTRAINING ORDER 2</u>

<u>IN LOVE WITH A CONVICT</u>

<u>Coming Soon</u>

BONDED BY BLOOD 2

BOW DOWN TO MY GANGSTA

Rise to Power 3